KALEIDOSCOPE

Kaleidoscope

Dark Tales
Derrick R. Lafayette

An Imprint of Joshua Tree Press LLP
Lexington, Massachusetts

ISBN: 978-0-9840369-9-8
LCCN: 2023903242

First Edition

Cover Design: Arash Jahani
Interior Design: Sophie Hanks

This is a work of fiction. The characters, situations and environments are a product of the author's imagination. Any resemblance to people, places or things in reality is utterly coincidental.

Printed in the United States of America

Fictional Cafe Press is the book publishing division of
The Fictional Cafe, an online 'zine.
https://www.fictionalcafe.com/

To my daughter Nova

Kaleidoscope

Dark Tales

Derrick R. Lafayette

A Fictional Cafe Press Book

"One night in September 1928, the broadcaster (BBC) devoted all seven studios in its Savoy Hill headquarters to a live modernist sound experiment, "Kaleidoscope," during which more than a hundred musicians, engineers, and actors performed "A Rhythm Representing the Life of a Man from Cradle to Grave."

— "London Calling" by Sam Knight, the *New Yorker*, April 18, 2022, p. 23.

https://genome.ch.bbc.co.uk/94d46c7c7a4747fa921a6fa81cb5d0d3

THE DARK TALES

THE ODDITY OF JO BOBBY
AND THE SEVEN DOORS

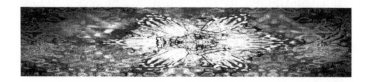

THE WILD WEST was a mysterious place at the best of times. Tales of la llorona roaming the lakes looking for the children she murdered can be heard in the same breath as the story of silver heels, looking for a dance partner who can look upon her horribly scarred face. But there is another myth told down in the backwoods of Tennessee: the story of the seven doors. Some say the seven doors are portals to the gates of hell.

Others say they force those who open them to witness their past crimes. But all say the seven doors are guarded by a creature not of this world, and very few are lucky enough to escape alive.

"You Bobby-Jo?" The question was posed by a balding man in his late forties, his skin cracked like old leather from too many days in the sun. A sweat-stained shirt, once dark brown, stretched over a sizable potbelly, stopping an inch or two above the worn gun belt strapped to his waist.

The man being asked considered the question from the wicker chair where he was sitting. August 9, 1830, was the hottest day the town of Wormwood, Tennessee, had ever seen. Rather than take one step out into the summer heat, most inhabitants were sleeping through the hottest part of the day, but the man being questioned was sitting on the wraparound porch of his Colonial-style blue-and-white house, a glass of iced tea in one hand. Tall, lean, with a nose sharp enough to cut stone, his deep-set eyes were so dark they were almost black.

"I'm Jo Bobby. What can I do for you, stranger?"

"Sonny and me"—the potbellied man dropped a large hand onto the scrawny shoulder of the boy standing by his side—"have been looking for a man what matches your gen'ral description and goes by the name of Bobby-Jo. Ain't that right, Sonny?"

"Sure is." Sonny bobbed his head in agreement, his dark eyes on the glass in Jo Bobby's hand. Bronze-skinned with the black, shoulder-length hair of someone with American Indian blood, he was no taller than the man's navel and three times as dirty. "Bobby-Jo sounds sim'lar to Jo Bobby, don't you think, Charlie?"

"Sounds similar to me." Charlie dropped a hand to one of the six-shooters he wore at his waist.

Jo Bobby regarded the two people in front of him calmly and took a sip from the iced tea in his hand. "You're fools if you think you can kill me and collect your bounty."

Charlie pulled back the hammer on his gun. "If you think I can't shoot an unarmed man a dozen feet away, you're the fool."

The gunshot blast rang throughout the sleepy town, startling the birds roosting in the trees. A gunshot blast so loud that the nearby sheriff, prune-skinned with a handlebar white mustache, woke up in his bed with a start, adjacent to a snoring whale of a woman who wasn't his wife.

"What the hell . . ." The sheriff reached for his gun holster, cupping his gleaming silver pride and joy hanging lazily off his bedpost, and swung out of bed, naked as a jaybird. "Betsy!" he barked and prodded at the mound of a woman who was not his wife. "Where in thunder are my pants?"

Across town Jo Bobby was knocked backwards out of his wicker chair by the gun blast, window glass smashing on the wooden porch boards. When Charlie stretched his sunburnt neck to see the corpse he had just created, it was positioned facedown, ass heavenward. He flexed his legs, looking at the tattered moccasins that'd been on his feet so long they were more patch than shoe. In contrast, his eyes glanced back at the leather cowboy boots on Jo Bobby that were almost brand new . Charlie kicked off his old moccasins, revealing his calloused and bruised ground stompers. Journeyman's feet, as if he'd been walking his entire life. Charlie quickly yanked the boots off the previous owner's feet and stuffed his raven's claws into the cowboy boots. They fit like a glove.

"So far, so good," he muttered.

Sonny eyed the spilled iced tea on the porch and licked his dry, cracked lips. "You coulda asked him to put down the glass afore you shot him," he said wistfully.

Charlie let his hand fall into Sonny's head of thick black curls. He was a young'un by young'un standards. Charlie grabbed a fistful of his hair and yanked. Sonny winced. "Show me that reward poster," he said. "Somethin' don't feel right about this one."

Obediently, Sonny fished out a crinkled "Dead or Alive" poster from his pocket, no bigger than a polished stone on a bolo tie. In the time it took him to unfold it, a salamander crawled over Charlie's boot and died from the taxing heat.

"Give it here." Charlie impatiently snatched up the picture of the supposed Bobby-Jo and held it against the piercing sunlight, squinting. "He look the same to you?" Charlie said, shifting the poster side to side.

"I thought so," Sonny muttered, rubbing his head. Charlie maneuvered Jo Bobby's body with a foot now covered in smooth stolen leather to get a look at his face. "Prolly gonna be hard to tell now," Sonny continued. "You shot him in the face, Charlie. You always gotta shoot 'em in the face, huh, Charlie?"

Charlie shrugged, poking the dead man again with his boot. "I was aiming for his chest."

He tried to compare the bullet-faced Jo Bobby with the poster. Nowhere in the universe could you find two more completely different people. It was like comparing an apple to a bullfrog. Different in race, size, even their noses: Jo Bobby's nose was square, while the man on the poster had a hooked nose, the type that'd been broken a few times over. The type that belonged to a disrespectful mouth.

"Well, shit," Charlie cursed and swatted Sonny on the back of the head. "I thought you said this was Bobby-Jo!"

"I can't read," Sonny whimpered. "It looked like him . . . or I thought it did."

Charlie went to let go of Sonny's hair, except he wasn't holding it anymore. It was sweaty, full of dandruff. He wiped his hand on his old buckskin jacket. "Won't get any reward off of this poor sonabitch." He scowled, gave Sonny a half-hearted smack on the back of the head. "Well, boy, sometimes you get, sometimes you get got. Sonny, go inside. You know what to look for, don't cha?"

"Sure do, Charlie." A large shadow of himself spread on the front porch as the day moved closer toward noon, the sun looming over Sonny. He lifted his poncho and sprinted up the small flight of steps. As he opened the front door, Sonny was stopped dead in his tracks at what he saw: a decanter riddled with condensation, brimful of golden tea, sitting on a short glass table. He licked his chapped and peeling lips greedily. The sight of the thirst-quenching tea widened his dark eyes, which had seen more than most young'uns. Manifest destiny was a few sandwiches short of a picnic. But it wasn't every day Sonny saw golden bliss. The liquid reflected in his pupils. He was salivating when suddenly the decanter spoke to him.

"Been a long few days on the road, Sonny? How about a refreshing cool glass of Bobby-Jo's famous iced tea?" the decanter whispered in echoes as droplets strolled down the side of the glass.

"So he is Bobby-Jo?" Sonny asked, mesmerized by the cool drops on the glass.

"What? He's Bobby-Jo?" a confused Charlie yelled from outside.

"That's what the iced tea said," Sonny responded.

"Mike Lee's in there? Sonofabitch stole my mule." Charlie came barging into the place with his gun out.

The door slammed closed behind them on its own, but neither man nor child noticed.

"Where's Mike?" Charlie demanded, looking around.

"I got a bullet with his name on it."

"No, Charlie," Sonny explained, "the iced tea. The iced tea said Jo Bobby was Bobby-Jo."

Charlie looked at Sonny sideways. He'd been staring at this dirty child's face for his whole existence, but just then he saw himself in the boy. An odd likeness, like hearing your speaking voice versus how it sounds in your head. He shook off the absurd notion and scanned the front room. Mounted deer and bear heads hung on opposite walls with a "Hail Yankee" area rug in the center.

"The heat got you talkin' to inadament objects again, Sonny? What I tell you about that? I know you Indians speak to lots of spirits, but that ain't one of 'em, boy."

"Are inadament things like animals?" Sonny asked. "Cuz I remember you said Mama used to talk to wolves."

"Inadament things ain't animals. They just things." Charlie pushed back what was left of the hair on his forehead. "I never seen her talking to no iced tea, just wolves." Charlie paused, then admitted, "Not after she smoked the pipe. It don't count."

"It spoke to me, Charlie; on Christ it did," Sonny insisted.

Charlie snorted and handed Sonny one of his guns. "Go on, get your drink, ya batty child. Anything else starts talking, you shoot it dead. I'm going upstairs and see if there's anything worth taking."

"You want a drink before you go?" Sonny asked.

Charlie smiled and ruffled the boy's filthy hair. "Nah, you can have the talking drink all to yourself."

The boy didn't need to be told twice. He lifted the decanter up to his mouth and began gulping down iced tea so fast it splashed onto his filthy shirt.

"You're welcome." Charlie shook his head, smiled, and stalked his way to the front of a spiral staircase in the majestic living room. He took each step bowlegged. Before him was a portrait of Jo Bobby riding a black horse through a flaming circle, holding a six-shooter. Underneath it read:

Houston 1823 Joseph Bobbington the Third

"Well, la-dee-dah," Charlie scoffed and proceeded up the staircase. "Looks like you got soft living in this fancy house. If you had spent less time drinking iced tea, maybe you'd still be alive and I'd be the one lying in the dust." He kicked at the wall with Jo Bobby's stolen boots. "But you ain't. You got soft and me and my boy are going to take as much as we can afore the law arrives."

Downstairs, Sonny put down the empty decanter with a happy sigh and sprawled on the ground, his belly protruding from underneath his tiny shabby shirt. His head rolled back, dangling in fulfillment.

"Had enough, Sonny?" the decanter whispered.

"I ain't suppose to talk to you. You inadament object and all. And I ain't crazy. I more sane than Charlie, that's for sure. He can't talk to spirits at all."

"There's more than just tea in this big ol' house, Sonny," the decanter responded.

Sonny raised his eyebrows, looked down, and rubbed his belly.

"Like what?"

"Like gold, Sonny."

The pristine spiral staircase seemed endless as Charlie pressed on, looking more and more bowlegged as his feet began to ache in his new boots. After twenty minutes and ten flights, he resembled a walking horseshoe. *How big is this house anyway?* he wondered. It hadn't looked to be more than two stories from the outside. Charlie looked back over his shoulder, wondering if he could call out to Sonny. But the only thing he could see was an infinite stream of stairs. Charlie picked up his foot and noticed a strange crack in one of the steps. It was V-shaped, and appeared to be spreading. Five minutes later he walked past the same crack. Charlie exhaled hard and continued to climb. "Should've drank that spooked tea when I had the chance."

Charlie was panting heavily when he finally approached the stairwell rail at the top and flopped onto the carpeted landing. His sweat had changed his light brown shirt to a dark gray and he coughed hard from tobaccy-scarred lungs. His gun belt was cutting into his potbelly, the result of too much cooked bison, and

Charlie unbuckled it, casting his gun aside as he inhaled the musty air. His feet felt as if they were covered in blisters and he kicked them off, one of his boots slipping off and tumbling down the mountain of stairs. Charlie watched it go, too tired to react.

"I'll get it on the way down," he mumbled to himself, buckling his gunbelt around his waist and getting to his feet.

The top floor was covered with an immaculate white carpet, untouched, brand-new. In front of him was a row of numbered rooms with lavender blue doors stretching the entirety of the corridor with strange painted-on windows at the end of the hall. There were seven doors in all, but the only number Charlie recognized was 1. He squinted his eyes at the puzzling sight, then tiptoed unsteadily with his one bare foot to the door. Charlie slowly placed his ear on it and pulled back the hammer on his pistol, listening for sounds within. After a moment, he was aware of a low muttering noise from the other side, indescribable at first. He pressed his ear harder against the door. The sound bubbled up, resembling virtuoso banjo music.

"Hmm, banjo can't be playing itself," he muttered and put a bullet through door number one.

"What ya shooting at now, Charlie?" Charlie flinched and spun around to see Sonny running up the long winding staircase, holding Charlie's forgotten boot. "Got ya boot by the way," he said, and Charlie noticed with envy the boy was barely out of breath. "Why're y'all sweaty?"

"How . . . how the heck you get up here so quick?" Charlie demanded.

Sonny looked at him, his dark eyes perplexed. "It ain't but a flight, Charlie. I coulda walked it backwards."

Charlie hobbled to the stairwell and looked down. Instead of the endless stairwell he had seen before, the first floor was clearly visible.

"Must be getting old." Charlie wiped thick sweat from his brow, and reaching into his back pocket, pulled out a scarred silver flask and took a deep swig.

"Eww." Sonny winced. "Ain't that scamper juice boiling hot, Charlie?"

Charlie scowled and took another swig. "Real men drink hot scamper juice, not fancy iced—"

"Charlie! Look!" Sonny cried. "I don't believe it!" A latent memory in Sonny's mind was sparked when he took notice of the seven doors on the second floor. Sonny had a flashback of his mother flipping through an old children's book, her brown skin reflected in the embers of a nearby burning fire. He smiled widely, as Charlie prepared another shot of both flask and pistol.

"The Seven Doors, Charlie, remember?"

"What the heck you talking, boy? Get yo' gun out," Charlie said, putting away the flask. He indicated the door that he had put a bullet into. "There's someone in there playing the banjo."

"You scared of a banjo, Charlie?"

"'Course not, Sonny, just some addlebrained fool who keeps playing long after someone shoots a hole in the door. You don't hear it?"

Sonny cocked his head, listening. "You got it wrong, Charlie," he said, shaking his head. "It's the Seven Doors, the old children's story. We in a fairy tale, Charlie."

Charlie peered into the hole he had shot through the door. Inside it was pitch black, with a small spotlight shining down on a floating banjo playing itself. Musical notes and treble clefs waltzed around it in midair. He blinked hard, but the image never changed. He pulled out the flask and took another swig of hot whiskey.

"I think you right, Sonny. How does the fairy tale go?"

Sonny shrugged. "Don't know, Charlie. I 'member the pictures though. A fat woman, a horse, an old sheriff, pretty ladies, and some other stuff. Guess I can't 'member now. Funny how when you try to 'member and just can't, huh, Charlie?"

"Pretty ladies like real ladies, or . . . ?"

"There was a picture of a big man wielding a six-shooter jumping through flames . . ." Sonny scratched his head thoughtfully. "But he was at the end."

"The end, huh?" Charlie thought of the portrait of Jo Bobby he'd passed on the way upstairs. "Must be a coincidence," he muttered to himself.

A hint of horse sweat plunged into the thick nose hairs of the sheriff as he galloped to Jo Bobby's estate. His whale of a not-wife was a tagalong his horse could've done without. Much to his surprise, Jo Bobby was leaning back in his wicker chair, unharmed, barefoot, drinking a glistening glass of iced tea. The sheriff dismounted from the poor horse and placed his boots on the hot ground.

"Morning, Jo."

"Morning, Sheriff."

"You heard any gunshots this morning? A particularly loud one? Louder than most, I mean. I've been checking around with folks to see if anyone knows where it came from."

"No, sir, can't say I have."

"Uh-huh." The sheriff eyed Jo Bobby. He'd hardly spoken to the man in the handful of years he'd been a resident of Wormwood. Truth be told, he hadn't wanted to. Jo Bobby was just plain unnerving. "Anything out the ordinary going on?"

Jo Bobby smiled and his black eyes met the sheriff's, sending shivers down the sheriff's spine. "No, sir, can't say they is."

The sheriff twisted his mustache, his keen eyes scanning the area. Something felt wrong, but he just couldn't put his finger on it. He suddenly caught sight of Charlie's discarded moccasins lying in the dirt and strode over to pick them up.

"You ain't sasafrassing me, is you, boy?" he asked, waving the moccasins in the air. "Why would someone leave a pair of shoes in front of your house?"

Jo Bobby shrugged, his dark eyes sly. "How would I know? The heat makes some men do strange things."

"Bullshit." The sheriff unsnapped his gun holster and granted the shining weapon its first appearance of the day. "Who was here? Where is he now? Did you shoot him?"

"Can't say I—" His sentence lost merit when the *clack!* of the sheriff's pistol hammer rang into the August air. "That your wife, Sheriff? She looks awfully parched. Care for some iced tea?"

"Step off your porch and ease over here. Something don't feel quite right."

"By all means, Sheriff," Jo Bobby complied as he lifted himself off the wicker chair. Jo Bobby walked slowly off his porch toward the sheriff. Despite the mounting sun, his body cast no shadow. The large woman panted heavily, all the while strewn over the back of the horse like a saddle, her heaving bosom catching Jo Bobby's gaze. With a wave of his hand, a floating decanter of iced tea manifested itself, bouncing in midair toward her.

Hee-Haw! A sharp kick from the horse's hind legs slid the heavy woman forward and the horse bucked down the dirt path, charging to get away from Jo Bobby.

Jo Bobby shook his head, a small disparaging smile on his face. "Am-na-mals are always the first to know."

Fright swept across the sheriff's face. He was unable to look back at his long-gone horse and overweight not-wife. He aimed the gun at Jo Bobby, his pistol shaking in his hand like beans in a can.

"What are you?"

A huge, oceanic shadow developed from behind Jo Bobby. It stretched the borders of his entire house and shrouded the whole estate in darkness. The trigger was immediately pulled on the gleaming silver pride and joy in the sheriff's hand. A thin flagpole jutted out the barrel and a piece of cloth unraveled with the word BANG on it in big red letters.

"So, how 'bout that iced tea, Sheriff? Awfully hot out here, ain't it? Don't worry 'bout ol' girl. You ain't got need of her."

Meanwhile, inside the house . . .

"I say we go through this one first," Charlie said, pointing at door number one. "If we want to loot this place, we can't have anyone alive calling for help."

"This job was supposed to be about collecting a bounty," Sonny said. "Now you want the law on our backs for killin' two innocent people?"

Charlie considered this. "Fine, we leave this door alone. And if anyone pokes their head out I'll tie them up," he said. "They won't be dead but they'll stop that goddanged banjo music."

"What banjo music? I still don't hear nothin'." Sonny cocked his head toward the door. "You sure you ain't going soft in the head? Maybe I should choose the door."

Charlie glared. "Listen here, you wet-behind-the-ears whelp, I'm as sane as I ever was. I'm the adult, and *I* say which door we go through first."

Sonny took a step back toward the stair railing and held Charlie's boot over the edge. "All right, you're in charge. But if the law shows up, you're going to have to run from them in one boot."

"Why you little . . ." Charlie took an uneven step forward. "I outta tan yore hide." He caught sight of what lay behind Sonny, the stairs beyond the railing seeming to go on forever again. Charlie wondered how long it would take to walk down and retrieve his boot and get back up the stairs. Better to let the boy have his say than to waste time. "We'll draw straws for it," he said, scanning the hallway. "Just need to find a twig or somethin'."

Sonny held out a fist. "Or . . . we could rock-paper-scissors for it."

Charlie scowled. "That's a kid's game."

Sonny shrugged. "All right. Waste time looking for something to use for a straw. I think I saw a broom closet downstairs."

Charlie's scowl deepened. "Fine, I'll play your kid's game. And I'm whumping your butt proper."

Two fists shook up and down rhythmically, stopping at the same time. The younger hand extended two fingers. The older kept a balled fist.

"Rock beat scissors!" exclaimed Charlie, a satisfied smirk on his face. "I told you I'd whump you at this kid's game."

"Rats!" pouted Sonny, as he stuffed his hands under his armpits.

"So, we did it fair and square and now I get to choose the door."

"Just don't shoot nothing in the face inside the room." Sonny scowled.

Charlie did his best to decipher which number looked the most attractive as he crept up and down the corridor. He tilted his head at the door with a 3.

"Sorta looks like those sideways bosoms, eh, Sonny?"

Sonny blushed. He was old enough to have seen a few of the women Charlie had visited in the brothels, but young enough to still be embarrassed. "Just open the door, Charlie."

Charlie watched the reflection of his ragged hand closing in on the golden knob. A shooting sensation of unbelievable cold ran up his arm and down to his hips. He danced involuntarily for a moment, much to Sonny's amusement.

"Quit laughing." Charlie scowled. "Was the house that done it," he said and twisted the knob. A wall of snow avalanched out and knocked him flat. Before he could utter a sound, a ferocious-looking, stark-white wolf leaped atop the snow pile Charlie was buried under, growling. Its luminescent crystal-blue eyes landed on Sonny, who whipped out his small pistol.

"Charlie! Don't move or you're done for!" Heavy frost emitted from the wolf's powerful jaws, and he snarled, his canines showing. "I'll shoot! I've shot things before, I'll do it again!" threatened Sonny, as he clutched the pistol in both hands.

The wolf, unfazed, slowly crept toward Sonny. A familiarity swept through him, gazing deeper into the abyss of the wolf's eyes. Flashbacks of his mother and Charlie. The aroma of crackling aged firewood, the clatter of horseshoes, and tribal battle chants all charged into his brain. Sonny's eyes rolled in his head and he fell backwards. Charlie's gun erupted from beneath the snow, followed by his arm, then the rest of him.

"Goddamn wolf!" Charlie shouted, as he let two more bullets fly at the animal.

The white wolf dodged, splitting into two identical wolves. Charlie unleashed three more bullets. The force shook snowflakes from its matted fur, inadvertently manifesting six more wolves. The newly formed pack rushed him and a schoolgirl's scream escaped from Charlie's mouth as he turned to flee: "AIYEEEEE!"

To his surprise, rather than attacking, the entire pack ran past him, out into the hall, scratching on the first door until they had created a sizable hole. The self-playing banjo danced out, followed by a string of waltzing music notes and treble clefs.

"I gotta quit drinking scamper juice," muttered Charlie, as the fantastical scene danced past him.

The wolves stood up on two legs and danced with the banjo, descending down the stairs and out of sight. The pathway downstairs instantly filled with solid, hard snow, trapping him and Sonny on the top floor. Two doors opened; only five doors left. Charlie glanced at door number two as a small flame sprouted out the keyhole. Charlie jerked back.

"Shit! There's a dragon in that one!" he cursed.

"Charlie?" Sonny muttered, as he raised himself from the floor. "Where am I? What happened?"

Charlie helped Sonny to his feet. "Sonny! You see the dancing wolves too? Dancing with the banjo?"

"Huh?" Sonny looked at him groggily.

"What the hell is this place?" In a panic Charlie reached for his silver flask, but instead a small bouquet of colorful flowers whipped out from the same pocket. "Sonny, what part of the story are we in?"

"Huh?" Sonny was still in a daze.

Charlie shook him roughly. "Sonny! The dang fairy tale, what part is this?"

"What you talking about, Charlie?" Sonny spoke the words, but the voice that came out was Jo Bobby's.

"Jo Bobby?" Charlie asked in disbelief.

"Enjoying my boots, Charlie?" Sonny's mouth curved into a smirk. "Can't take a man's shoes without walking a man's miles."

"Is that why I'm seeing these things? I'll give 'em back."

"A bit too late for that, Charlie." Sonny laughed. "Now go on, open door number two."

Loud, obnoxious sounds squeaked from the floorboards as Charlie moved closer to the door. *Squeak . . . Squeak . . .* The fire spewed out even more ferociously. He clamped his hand on the knob. The smell of searing flesh wafted under his nose.

"Ahh! Christ!" Charlie yelled, as he twisted the knob and opened the door.

Behind door number two was a forest with many moving parts. Shadows, horses clattering, and chaos all about.

"Look familiar, Charlie?" Sonny spoke, still with Jo Bobby's voice.

"The Cherokee tribe?"

"I been waiting for you, Charlie. You walked right into my game."

"Game? What are you talkin' about?"

Inside door number two, under a crescent moon, teepees were set ablaze in a dark forest masked with dirt plains. Brightly colored feathers adorned white horses upon which the Indian chieftains sat, clashing head-on with white men dressed in uniform. The sound of gunshots rang out as war ensued. Torches were set to erect totem poles. Madness raged all about the small village.

"Take 'em all out! Women, children, every last one of 'em!" yelled the Yankee captain as he unsheathed a long sword with a golden handle.

Arrows pierced the flesh of the white men, felling many. Others returned fire with old pistols. The smell of gunpowder filled the clean western air.

"Look familiar, Charlie?" Jo Bobby whispered from the door.

A cloud of smoke was all that remained when the white men finally won. Dead bodies lay on the grass. The Yankee captain galloped over to a young Charlie and patted him on the back.

"Hmm, you did good with this one, huh?"

Charlie looked down at his shaking hand. In front of him was a young woman in buckskins lying lifeless in the grass. A free-falling, lone snowflake descended on

Charlie's cheek and infused itself in an unrestrained tear.

"They said that blizzard would be coming soon. We done what was needed. Move out back to camp, boys!" the Yankee captain cheered as the brigade followed suit and exited the massacre they had created.

Everyone left except Charlie, who remained on the blood-soaked battlefield, weeping quietly.

Charlie watched his younger self straighten as his ears picked up another sound, a mewling cry coming from the fallen woman. Cautiously, he approached his victim, lifting her body and rolling her onto her side. A two-year-old Sonny blinked up at him from inside a woven cradleboard, then he suddenly smiled and gurgled, his tiny hands reaching out to grasp Charlie's thumb.

"Uh . . . hey there, sonny . . ." Charlie watched as the younger Charlie glanced around to ensure that the troops were gone. Night was falling and the snow was getting thicker. Alone, the small boy would not last the night. "I'm sorry . . ." Younger Charlie took out his gun and pointed it at the squalling boy. "But trust me, this is a kindness."

Young Charlie froze, his finger on the trigger as he spotted six wolves in the distance. Man and beast locked eyes, watching each other as snow fell harder from the night sky. The essence of a supernatural, or spiritual, occurrence echoed through their exchange of stares, and Charlie remembered the extraordinary feeling he had felt that night. As if the wolves had told Charlie to spare the child. He watched as the younger Charlie bent down to pick up Sonny inside the cradleboard and a crude book made from bark dropped to the ground. The cover read "The Seven Doors."

"Starting to clear up, ain't it, Charlie?" Jo Bobby whispered through Sonny's voice.

Charlie stood motionless, an ancient, buried memory displayed like a moving painting. His face was stone still.

"Open door seven." Sonny spoke with Jo Bobby's voice.

Without hesitation, Charlie made his way to the last door. Inside, Charlie could see a forest, and beyond was a small camp. Tents tilted and campfires were doused as the snowfall grew heavier. Flags with single stars on tall posts flopped in the wind. A young Charlie looked down on them from a hill's edge, the cradleboard stuffed with young Sonny and the "Seven Doors" book at his side. He peered into the innocent young Sonny's dark brown eyes. The infant yawned heartily and grasped Charlie's pinky with his tiny fist.

"If I go down there with a papoose, they go'n to kill him," young Charlie murmured to himself. "And if I desert them, they'll hunt me down and kill us both."

Pressing against a few shrubs to act as a canopy, the cradleboard tucked beneath it, young Charlie climbed down the small hill as quietly as possible, pistol in one hand and a knife in the other.

"Was the plan to kill them all?" Sonny through Jo Bobby's voice asked from the border of the door, peeking into the living flashback. Both watched as one of the soldiers noticed young Charlie's approach and was immediately killed before he could make a sound.

"At first . . . but a pistol with six bullets won't hold 'gainst a troop. So . . ."

"You decided to burn them."

Charlie seized a thick log from the fire and tossed it onto the closest tent. The flame caught and grew, spreading fast until the entire canvas was consumed. Young Charlie tossed burning logs at two other tents, watching as they, too, went up in flames, spreading to other tents in close proximity. The sound of cheers and a distant banjo playing was replaced with shouts of fear and panic. A wall tent caught fire nearby and became lively as the soldiers rushed outside. The captain appeared from the emerging group wearing tattered white pajamas, wielding a banjo.

"Charlie! What the hell you doin', boy?"

His six-shooter lost two bullets. The Yankee captain owned them now inside his chest.

Young Charlie waved the gun at his old comrades, hate fueling their eyes with the fire adding to the effect. Taking his knife, Charlie slashed through the ropes tying down the soldiers' mounts. The panicked animals fled, leaving the men stranded behind. Young Charlie seized the reins of the last horse tethered nearby and mounted, galloping away.

The fire raged across the campground and melted the first layers of skin off the heavy sleepers. Even the weapons were destroyed, the fire burning the wooden stocks and melting the metal, rendering them useless. Young Charlie snatched up the sleeping Sonny and raced away, ignoring the flames and chaos behind him. The number seven door closed.

"The ones who survived died later that month from the blizzard," Sonny said. "Hefty bounty out on your head after that. You wasn't Charlie no more. Nah, you's the 'Coward Yankee Killer' now. A lone wolf with a cub."

"What was I s'pose to do?"

Sonny shrugged. "Plenty of men wouldn't have thought twice about whether to leave an infant to die rather than turn their back on their own race."

"Plenty of men never found themselves talkin' to

wolves," Charlie returned. "Don't matter anyhow; it's done now."

"You don't have regrets?" Sonny asked.

Charlie reached out and ruffled Sonny's filthy hair. "Not one," he said.

Sonny shook his head. "You're a rare one, Charlie," he said with Jo Bobby's voice.

With the snap of a finger, Charlie and Sonny were transported back to the porch of the blue and white house. Jo Bobby leaned in his wicker chair, drinking cold iced tea on the hottest day Wormwood had ever seen. He nodded to Charlie, who realized the cowboy boots were back on his feet. Sonny blinked and looked around in surprise.

"Charlie? How did we get down here? Why does my mouth taste purple all 'a sudden?" Sonny queried in his own voice.

Charlie nodded back to Jo Bobby, then looked down on Sonny.

"We was just leaving, Sonny. Let's go," Charlie said.

"Tell him the truth 'bout himself, Charlie," said Jo Bobby. "A man knowing where he come from is the gold mine of his soul. That's the whole point of this."

"Gotcha. Say, so you dead . . . or?"

"Me? Well, hard to say . . ." Jo Bobby took a sip of sweet tea. "I'm someone who existed beyond the rules your kind grew up on. If we meet again, maybe I'll tell ya. Best get on now, before I change my mind." Jo Bobby tossed a tin canteen full of tea to Sonny. It was covered in blue woolen cloth. The sound of stagecoach wheels broke the tense concentration taking place in Charlie's head, trying to figure out what the hell it all meant. The stage was driven by two horses. A beautiful woman with thick blonde curls, wearing a sapphire dress, was holding the reins. Charlie smiled for the first time in ages.

"Pretty ladies, Sonny," elbowed Charlie with a grin.

"You boys need a ride?" The blonde driver leaned forward slightly to show off an impressive bosom. "We are heading down to Nashville, could use some feller company for protection and all. It's just me and my sisters. We got room for you and the young'un."

"Haven't I seen ya'll before?" Sonny blurted out, scratching his head.

"Doesn't matter." Charlie was already walking quickly toward the stagecoach. "Got a few days at least to get acquainted if we don't, and reacquainted if we do."

THE PROBLEM

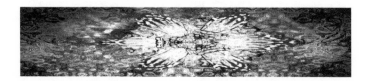

THE CANDIDATE'S SKIN TURNED GRAY.

"He's been rejected," the young woman murmured to the older man beside her. The candidate's skeleton had become visible when his life force divorced him. A mist of teal swirled and burst into tiny stars, which dimmed on the descent. A swinging lantern squeaked in the silence. Nova, her dark hair hanging in wisps around her narrow face, shook her head in defeat, murmuring quiet words of despair. Her father's hand glowed as he slowly inserted his palm into the dead body's rib cage and grabbed onto an object. It was cold and diamond-sized, pulsating like a heart.

"Is that what my death is going to look like, Father?" Nova whispered as her father slipped the soul into a pouch.

"We're supposed to be bringing life," Logan responded. "And no. These are peculiar circumstances."

Nova stuck her head out the stagecoach door. She saw objects moving in the night. Shapes forming in the distance. Some bipedal. Some not touching the ground at all.

"Creatures of the dark are approaching," she reported. "We need to move on."

The smell of wet earth and sage filled the carriage. The two horses outside, tired of the weather, nibbled listlessly at blades of grass around the loose and busted-up wheels of the stagecoach. The dirt road ahead was uncharted. On the torn map Nova traced a route between forests and splotches of blood on the parchment. Logan gathered the recently deceased's belongings: a compass, a letter, two silver coins, and a dull blade.

"Cover your face or you'll grow sick from the cold," Logan suggested as they entered the driver's box. He touched her sleeveless overgarment. The material was damp from the weather outside. "You need new clothes."

"Mother makes new clothes out of the old."

"When Mother wakes up, I'll have her make you a wardrobe, and cook us a feast, and regale us with her singing."

"If she ever does."

Nova's dark eyes clouded slightly as she remembered, if it were not for her mother, she and her father would not be on this journey. Visions of the past tormented her: a body floating in the water, Mother struggling in the river as she fought against a creature that seemed to be made of sunlight, Mother screaming as she was bound within the living bark of the Melancholy Tree, Mother's sleeping face surrounded by leaves . . .

"How far is the next town?" Logan asked.

"I don't know where it is," Nova stuttered. "The map only shows more woods. Mountains very far away."

A howl that sounded more animal than man reached their ears. It doubled, quadrupled in the night air.

"Take these." Logan handed the reins to Nova.

He carefully went inside the stagecoach, placed his hand under the corpse, and rolled it outside into the mud. It barely made a noise as it landed.

"Less weight."

By morning, Nova was resting inside the stagecoach and Logan had taken them downhill to a town that wasn't on the map. His eyes were dark from lack of sleep. There were wooden houses, small farms, shops, and in the center a manor made of natural stone. He stopped next to an establishment with a photograph of an elixir in the window. He climbed off the stagecoach and placed his hand on its side. A silver aura briefly glowed. After a brief moment Logan knocked twice on the front door of the store, then turned the knob.

"I've just opened my store," the apothecary said. He was a young boy with a nest of brown hair, wearing a white tunic, a copper ring on each index finger. "Please, a moment to gather myself."

Logan pulled down his green hood, revealing his sun-beaten, lightly scarred, chiseled face with a salt-and-pepper beard. He glanced out at the stagecoach, then turned to the apothecary. "Take your time. I'm grateful to find you here. This town was not on my path. You see, my daughter and I—"

"No need," the apothecary interrupted him. "Personal affairs are personal affairs. And quite frankly, your map is terribly outdated."

Logan walked next to a wooden cabinet where glass jars rested at the top. On the shelves were various spices and herbs and incenses. In one whiff he was able to gather the scent of pepper, mint, and tobacco. He placed his face next to a peculiar glass jar filled halfway with a yellow substance. Inside was a small heart. He tapped the glass lightly. The heart reacted.

"It began as a concoction for gout. But the experiment took on a life of its own," the apothecary said as he took his place behind the register. "How can I be of assistance?"

"Thyme's to combat a cold brought about by the season. We're out of sage and lavender. I'll take some comfrey and licorice if you have it. I have two silver coins." Logan reached in his pouch and took out the dead man's currency.

"Which direction did you come from, traveler?"

"North."

"Any others on your road?"

Logan glanced around the store. "Only me."

"You plan to be out in the cold for long?"

Logan ignored the question. "Do you know where I can get any wool?"

The carriage was still parked when Nova opened her eyes. Light streamed through the windows, catching floating dust motes and turning them into gold.

"Hungry?" Logan presented her with smoked herring on a stick and a wool sweater. "You should change first," he advised and turned his head so she could take off the damp garments and slip into the new clothes.

"This undocumented town is better than our own." Logan smirked as he began to eat hard bread. "At least we'll be full by night."

"They will come again?" Nova inquired with a slight tremble in her voice as she bit into the herring.

"We have something from the netherworld. They'll want it back."

"Mother found it by the lake."

"Godhood came to her in his death. Death has now come for us."

"She's been sleeping ever since. Ever since she gave us the . . ."

"Until we can pass it on, they will hunt us to reclaim the soul."

"But . . ." Nova took another bite of the herring. "All the candidates are dead."

Logan unrolled a scroll and used his finger to go down the list of names. At the bottom, he pressed his nail into the scroll. Ink manifested at his fingertip and he checked off the name: Vicar Abel. He sat back hard in the seat and exhaled long. He knew Nova wouldn't say all that was on her mind. A trait of his own. Finished eating, she opened the door. Logan grabbed her hand.

"I wish to see the town," she protested, jerking her arm in his grip.

"Not alone."

"It's okay, Father, the sun will protect us."

On the soft dirt road they walked past various farmers and merchants. Nova gallantly skipped, having stretched her legs from the long journey in the stagecoach. Logan let his guard down upon noticing he was physically larger than every man nearby. On a pole at a fork in the path was a poster of a missing man. He was wearing cleric's robes. All the letters were in a foreign language.

"They believe in the false gods here?" Nova asked him.

Logan placed his face close to the poster. "Their faith might be what we need."

"I don't understand, Father."

Logan's hand glowed silver as he waved it over the words. Each alien symbol mutated into letters he understood. Once complete, he was able to read the man's name, and so was she. Nova's eyes narrowed.

"Vicar Abel. He is from here?"

"It would seem."

"Why didn't he mention it?"

"He was too excited to become the next Godhood."

"How sad."

They traveled east toward a road lined with devil grass. Horse-carts were headed in the opposite direction, driven by Herculean people with strange tattoos on their faces. Nova was unable to see through the steel bars of the cargo, but her instinct told her humans were inside.

Before she could voice her thoughts, they noticed the top of the natural-stone manor rising from below the hill.

"We're approaching the center of the city," Logan whispered while eyeing the space between the trees nearby, on the lookout for more Herculean men or runaway slaves.

"It's a temple, Father. Like I've seen in my books."

Acolytes were laughing and conversing loudly by the temple walls, dressed in robes of mustard yellow and blood red. Next to a stone pillar connected to a bridge was a priest in a robe of pristine white. His face bore tiny hairs jutting from his chin, and was younger than anyone else's around him. He smirked at the commotion before him. Some were flailing their arms, while others were stuffing coins into their purses.

"The book is clear on lineage. Being born into poverty is the will of Deus," one of them yelled out. He stroked his red beard hard as he spoke. "Vassals must capitalize. It is his will."

"A man born of blood and bone can change. Deus can speak and transform any of his children," another rebutted.

"Aye, but not one impure. To be fair, they have genetics I wish could be bought. I only grow fatter and balder." Red-beard laughed. "Scarcely worth a sixpence."

"A downhill journey of age," the priest said clearly, silencing the debate. "Let us partake of Communion."

They all took out small round wafers and raised golden goblets of wine. Logan and Nova walked reasonably close so they could make out the details of the ritual. Most of the acolytes noticed Nova first, then Logan. The priest pursed his lips.

"Spiritual cannibalism," Logan murmured to Nova as some of the acolytes turned their heads, watching the unfamiliar pair approach.

"Father and child. I see her in you and you in her," said the priest, leaning forward on the pillar. "Have you come for the word of Deus? Or has Deus spoken to you and led you to me? Lady Mallard takes in refugees of all types. We have no qualms about immigrants. All are welcome."

"Deus has spoken to both me and my daughter," Logan answered.

The priest chuckled. "Deus only accepts men."

"I don't wish to join you, but I require a meeting. May we talk in private? I believe we've crossed paths for a purpose which is beyond both of our reasonings."

The acolytes snickered among themselves. The priest waved his hand to control them.

"You are not from anywhere near here. There are, ah, steps to be taken. I appreciate your boldness. I imagine it has taken you far."

"Far enough to have met your father."

Gasps erupted amongst the crowd. One could hear the priest swallow his spit.

"I am not easily moved," he replied. "Especially by lies from a stranger's mouth."

"Vicar Abel is dead."

"My father died the moment he left the church."

"No." Logan raised the letter that had been in the dead man's clothes. His hand glowed silver around the parchment. "He died in my stagecoach last night while trying to inherit the soul of Godhood."

Inside the inner sanctum of the temple, Nova stood in a circular religious symbol carved into the floor. It resembled a serpent coiled on a cross. Around it was a design of various spheres and lines, puzzle-like. Logan glossed over the stained-glass paintings, not trying to figure out who was who. The priest swirled a goblet of wine, rubies encrusted around its brim.

"Nightfall. That's when the danger presents itself," the priest clarified. "And I'm a candidate?"

"You are one of a line of descendants of the world's greatest sorcerer," Logan said. "His soul was bequeathed to one of my family before the Darkness claimed him. Now they hunt us in an attempt to retrieve it."

"One of your family. Do you mean . . ." The priest pointed at Nova.

"No," Leeto answered. "My wife. She sleeps until we can find a worthy candidate to accept the soul and become a Godhood."

"And I am . . ."

"The last," Nova chimed in.

"And I can become God?" He sipped from his goblet.

"God*hood*," Logan corrected him. "An immortal who walks in the light. I'm sure your acolytes are surrounding the doors, but you have very little time. There won't be enough prayers to protect you from the shadows of the netherworld."

"I won't need anybody . . . eventually." The priest began undoing the buttons of his robe. "I imagine this power goes in the chest?"

Logan opened his satchel and took out the object. As his hand turned silver, it began to pulsate. He scoped the dimensions of the room, then nodded to Nova. Nova's index finger began to summon specks of dirt that glittered and formed miniature stars. A gravitational pull resting atop her nail. She turned her feet inward and began to dance. During her spins, rune symbols painted themselves in the air. Logan commanded one of the runes toward his face. A portal opened to reveal a figure. Beneath the hood of an obsidian-black robe, only a broad nose and topaz eyes could be seen. The priest drank what was left of his libation.

Logan kneeled. "The problem is resolved," he whispered in a language the priest could not understand.

"Do you pledge to relieve your essence, ensuring the resurrection of me?" Godhood asked the priest.

"Of which I am the head," the priest slyly remarked.

"Your life force will cease to be," Godhood replied, as the portal closed.

A scream echoed from outside the door. Nova looked out the window at the full moon, then down toward shadows slithering up the stone walls, seeping into the building. A giant skeletal hand covered by darkness reached inside, not bound by physical matter.

"Return the rest of him," the Dark Force uttered. "He rightfully belongs to us."

"Do it now, Father!" Nova commanded.

Logan grabbed Godhood's soul and approached the priest. The priest began to walk away from the pulsating thing.

"Wait, I want to reconsider the terms," said the priest as he unsheathed a small dagger with a golden handle. Moonlight licked the blade. "Will I cease to be?" he asked frantically, reaching behind himself for the door.

"You will be a conduit. Nothing more," Logan answered.

"I'm the last one! She said it. You need me." The priest slashed at the space between them. "I want control!"

Horns formed through the wall. The Dark Force's face protruded farther into the room. His jowl grazed the floor. Flaming eyes and wrinkles made tendrils of smoke. Nova created new runes to form a temporary shield. Two hands raised high, she struggled to hold it. The priest turned the knob on the door with his hand behind his back, trying to escape.

The hallway was a macabre scene of bodies strewn and splayed over the walls. Blood-soaked robes, gray flesh, and jewelry littered the floor. Tentacles of shadows were dragging the survivors into portals of amethyst.

"You've brought hell upon us!" the priest said as he darted down the corridor.

"I had no choice!" Logan called out as he pursued him. Over his shoulder he saw Nova, now on her knees, hands stiil up, palms open. One of the Dark Force's feet, long and flat with talons, penetrated the wall.

In the courtyard the priest stumbled through bramble, slicing with his dagger at anything near him, nicking a statue of one of the wise men from his dogma. At his feet, he felt a warm sensation. He looked down and noticed a giant mouth forming in the grass. He fled. The shadow-monster began to rise. Its head was enormous, its mouth two rows of jaws, its three legs on each side of its ill-shapen midsection churning. Suddenly, a tentacle of shadow wrapped around the priest's neck as he stepped on the entrance steps. His sandals dropped from his feet as it carried him into the air with the tightness of a noose.

Logan saw him dangling in the air. He curled his hand into a fist; a silver aura covered the priest's body and pulled it toward him. The tentacle didn't release its hold; the priest was unable to speak from the constriction on his neck. Veins throbbed in his head and his eyes filled with blood.

The moment Logan had the priest's body close to him, he pressed the soul directly into the man's chest. A tremendous light shone from the priest's eyes as Logan struggled to get his hand free.

Within the inner sanctum, the Dark Force hovered over a defeated Nova as her runes disintegrated in the air. His full form was an amalgam of mystical creatures, talons, tails, and appendages, with the face of a twisted elder days after death. He opened his mouth and vomited thick shadows that moved like tornadoes. Creatures rose from the ooze. Sharp claws grew from their small hands, and they began cutting at her legs.

"You are not who I am seeking!" the Dark Force said as more darkness leaked from his mouth. "But your pain will suffice."

Nova rolled to dodge the attacks and placed her hand on a pillar. The bricks inside melded together into one form, and a bright beam of sunlight flooded the entire room, blinding her.

"You have done as I asked and given my soul to a worthy candidate," said a voice, which was the source of the light. "Now I will fulfill my end of the bargain."

"My thanks," Nova whispered. She stood, wobbled, felt around for safety. A hand in a velvet glove touched her. Even shielding her eyes, all she could see was white with a silhouetted figure in black looking at her. Wings escaped from its sides; a hood covered its face. She heard Logan in the distance.

"Follow the sound of my voice," he said.

Nova backed away from the light, reaching behind her. As she moved, she saw the black figure manifest a war-hammer with enormous spikes on each end. It raised it high, pulling in a strong gust of wind, and slammed it down on the stone floor. All the shadow creatures transformed into black sand. The figure pounded the mighty war-hammer again and the Dark Force's foot was severed from his body. As the blinding light faded, Nova watched Godhood grab the Dark Force's neck.

"Eventually this body will cease to be! And your soul will dwell in the netherworld once again. Death is inevitable," the Dark Force screamed.

Godhood unhinged his jaw. His body parts expanded rapidly, making him over seven feet tall with disproportionate muscles. He opened his mouth and inhaled. The horns went in first, as the Dark Force tried to seep back into the natural stone of the temple. Godhood stretched his neck back and consumed all of the darkness in the room. He hunched forward momentarily. An arm jutted from his side, however, still bound to his skin and trapped in his stomach. Godhood put his velvet-gloved hand over the protruding arm and pushed it back into his body. A horn bulged from his neck, a foot from his chest. Godhood struggled to keep the Dark Force inside.

Logan's hand glowed silver as he placed it on Godhood's back. The Dark Force battled no more. Nova glanced at the corpses in the hallway, or at least what remained of them.

"We must leave before the townsfolk come." She tugged on Logan's shirt.

"The deed is done," Logan said to Godhood.

"You and yours have served me well," Godhood replied, placing a small bottle of golden liquid in Logan's hand. "As in the beginning, and now. My most loyal. Forgive your wife for stepping into your shoes."

"Praise be to Godhood." Logan kneeled and placed the bottle in his coat pocket.

A few meters from the river, Logan's wife was wrapped inside the Melancholy Tree, only the top half of her body showing a few inches from the trunk. Fig leaves decorated her hair. Below her navel branches were intertwined with her body, binding her to the Tree. She didn't seem to be in any pain and rested peacefully within the trunk, a smile on her face. Logan took out the small bottle, kneeled, and poured it into the grass below.

Inside their home, Nova caught her little brother who leaped into the air, excited for her return. He bombarded her with kisses on her cheeks and hugged her tight around the neck. An older woman who walked with the assistance of a wooden cane smiled at her.

"He wouldn't stop talking about you. You'd a think a boy would be more obsessed with his father, but not this one," the older woman said, before turning to a kettle and brewing tea.

The little brother's eyes were the size of the moon, itching to ask Nova a million questions in a single breath.

"What happened out there? Is Mother coming back with you? Where's Father? Did you travel by foot the entire way? Did you fight monsters?" the little boy inquired.

Nova smirked at him. "You want to hear the whole story?"

"Yes! From the beginning."

Nova settled herself by the fireplace, her little brother on her lap. "Well, the most powerful sorcerer in the world was poisoned with cursed bile. It damaged him so much that he collapsed into a river and floated downstream. Mother found his body near the shore while she was washing clothes. The sorcerer removed his soul from his body, placed it in Mother's hands, and whispered thirteen names to her. Then shadows grabbed his corpse and pulled it into the netherworld. When Father found Mother, she was being attacked by a sun creature who moved freely in the light. He bound Mother to the Melancholy Tree before Father beheaded him. Mother said all the names the sorcerer had told her before falling into a deep sleep. That night, the sorcerer went into Father's dream and told him to give his soul to one of his mortal descendants and in return he would give him the elixir to free Mother."

"Ohhhh." The little brother opened his mouth wide. "So what happened next?"

THE WITNESS

I SPENT THE ENTIRE DAY IN BED staring at
the white ceiling. If you stare at it long enough, it begins
to sweat. Mother always said I was an "overthinker."
When she remembered me, before Alzheimer's. Before
the inevitable change when we all wither. I never believed
it until now.

I scrolled through my phone searching for the app
that controls my life. Since my remote's been lost in
the abyss of my apartment, I needed it to tune in and
tune out. It was an ungodly hour. I could tell from the

pulsating tangerine glow of the streetlights on my white curtain blinds. During particular times in the night, they malfunctioned. I used to think microscopic cameras were inside snapping pictures of me. Aliens sending Morse code. Or, that I was subconsciously controlling it with my mind, trying to send myself a message from within. A myriad of paranoid fantasies. I take pills now. I'm better now. I don't think as much.

After sliding my feet into two-year-old brown slippers, I grabbed a bowl, a box of cereal, and a questionable bottle of milk. I sat near my oscillating fan, listening to the sound of my teeth crunching the cereal. Unsatisfied, I made some room on the floor by shifting dirty clothes and piles of unopened mail. I proceeded to do push-ups until my arms gave out. I did seven.

I took a shower and cleaned my bathroom immediately after. I scanned social media methodically, searching for rabbit holes. I played a game of chess against myself beneath a single light bulb hanging from the ceiling on a long electrical cord. Stalemate. Nothing worked. At the forefront of my mind was a recent memory. I saw something . . . and it wouldn't leave me alone.

After work last night, when I got on the bus I took a different route home. I spent the entire ride without people watching, which is instinctual for me. Except, lately, the eyes staring back caused me great panic. So I put my focus on the floor, the poles, empty seats, the ceiling. I watched my shoes grow, then missed my stop. My street slopes downhill, so I could see beyond the oasis of metropolitan life. I'm frightened by the roar of the living. I never bought into or wanted to enter the mainstream of modern existence. I tried once; it was an amicable breakup.

My mother would say that I transformed myself into a walking ghost. She was right—trauma transforms. I wished the world could pass through me. Unfortunately, bounded by the flesh, I found myself brushing past a group of degenerates near the lavender hue of a sex shop. Several types of hookahs, tall and small, were displayed behind the storefront glass.

I declined eye contact with the Muslim shopkeeper in the corner store when he handed me change for the items I'd purchased: a 40-oz. bottle of malt liquor, hand lotion, assorted candy bars. He commented on a stain on my gray hoodie that had been there for over a month. In response I nodded my head, and with the gracelessness of a snail found my way to the exit. The bell chimed above my head, and I entered the block that my home was built on.

Habitually, I keep my keys in my left pocket because I'm left-handed. But last night they were in my back pocket, with the change in my right. I forget why. There's a permanent fog in my short-term memory. When I began entering my apartment, momentarily I felt like a different person. Someone with a life worth living. The streetlights were still working.

A spotted black-and-white cat rubbed against my leg. In the backdrop of a star-filled night sky, one fell. The cough I'd nursed for a week disappeared. In my left pocket, I found a twenty-dollar bill. I decided to drag my newfound auspiciousness to the park.

Down one of the trails, I saw an old woman throwing pieces of bread on the ground. Two couples, reeking of marijuana, pointed at me, sniggered, and walked toward the edge of the street. I debated whether their laughter was real or not. While contemplating this, I located a space between the trees to be alone. Dragonfly nymphs cavorted in the still water by my feet. Through the leaves above I was just able to see the crescent moon. I twisted off the beer bottle's cap and drank to the loneliness. The passing of time was now measured in how much beer remained in the bottle. When it was nearly gone, and while still enveloped in the unnatural city silence, I saw it: a human-shaped object flying across the sky.

I dropped the bottle into the still water, knowingly contaminating it, then walked back to the path near the streetlights. Not a soul in any direction. It felt as if I'd entered the twilight of a dream. At the edge of degradation. I squeezed through the fence rails beneath the bridge, blocking off the huge lake that split the park in two. I watched it, whatever it was, fly by again. A blur.

An unwarranted laugh bubbled inside me. The thing dropped from the sky, creating ripples on the surface of the lake, and stopped, hovering a few feet away from me.

It was undulating and luminescent. I'd never seen such beauty. Its eyes were like jewels and its curves were as smooth as river stone. No defined features specified its sex; nevertheless, I haven't been able to sleep since. There were moments when I blocked out all external forces. Except at those times I wasn't aware I was communicating with the external world. My mouth moved for me.

"Are you sure you're not a cop?" the near-naked prostitute whispered into my ear. The smell of tobacco smoke and burnt plastic assaulted my nostrils.

"I need to relax."

"You want a motel? It's the best way without a car. Out here"—she scanned the inner city we both found ourselves in—"the streets have eyes."

"I don't do this often," I lied, but she saw through it, even with her fake eyelashes and mascara.

"Whatever helps you sleep, right?"

"That's my problem."

The motel was one I'd frequented before. I'd memorized the layout, the pricing, the filthiness of the pool. Lying on the bed, I watched the ceiling sweat. A faucet was abruptly turned off. A door creaked open. The silhouette of a woman's naked frame presented itself in the shadows. A stack of money occupied the corner of a desk. I was straddled.

"Do you need anything?" she asked, close to my ear. "Alcohol, drugs?"

"I don't think so."

The physical touch landed on dead limbs. She took notice and rolled over, sparked a cigarette. In the glow of the flame, I saw boredom tattooed on her face.

"No refunds. We can just lay here. Talk, I suppose." Her tone of voice grew brighter.

"I'd prefer that," I said.

She glanced at my crotch. "Happens more often than you'd think."

"I saw something." A confession escaped.

"Don't we all?" She offered a cigarette. "See stuff."

The following night, I began sketching furiously. On paper towels, napkins, the walls, any surface. I drew it. Different poses. Flying, swimming, holding my hand, angel wings. My voicemails were filling up from work messages I didn't care to hear. I was tired of pushing a broom, earning barely enough to pay for my prescriptions. The streetlight started to pulse again, sending me messages, ideas. I listened. I decided to reenter the park and retrace my steps.

The unnatural silence hugged me. I approached my spot between the trees. However, when I looked up through the leaves, there was no moon. I waited. The night grew colder. The frigid, cutting breeze awakened deep thoughts. Epiphanies. I felt as though I had spent too much time not making memories. Swathed in isolation.

"I've never seen you here before," a voice whispered near the path. "Are you waiting?"

"Yes," I answered loudly, approaching a homeless man sitting on the bench near the lake. "I need to see it again."

"Me too." He rubbed his beard and looked toward the sky. "What does it look like to you?"

"Something otherworldly."

"It spoke to me once."

"What did it say?"

The homeless man stretched his neck and sank his shoulders. "I don't know . . . I couldn't make out the language. I . . . I've been coming here ever since. Hoping to see it. Praying for it to speak again." The homeless man showed me a notebook filled with numbers and letters deciphered into half-finished sentences. He was decoding.

"How long?"

"Sixty-five days. Or six-hundred and five days. I'm not entirely sure."

Before long, the night transitioned to sunrise. I had cramps in my back from lying on the grass. I had let myself fall asleep. The homeless man was gone. A familiar jogger stared at me as she passed. I'd seen her before, but when? The shirt I slept in was a different color than I remembered. My stomach was angry. I left the park to return home.

There was a sixty-day eviction notice on my apartment door. Luckily my key still worked. I had ants crawling in my hair. I thought about the thing in the shower as accumulated dirt fell into the bathtub. When I looked at myself in the bathroom mirror, I realized I had lost weight. There was darkness in my eyes. Blotchiness on my skin. Pimples on my arms. The price of worship.

I collected the drawings. Lit a candle in the center. I kneeled before it. I prayed to it. Then I smudged the house with sage. Garbage occupied every corner of my living room. A stench of last week, or maybe last month? I grabbed a notebook and began writing the story of my first encounter. My handwriting was similar to the homeless man's. Scattered.

The next night, three inches of snow covered the ground. I waited for the streetlight to blink. With the drawings in my possession, I went to my place between the trees. A shadow moved next to the frozen rivulet that once was still water.

"It hasn't come," the homeless man said. There was a clear weight loss in his appearance, even under the heavy clothes. "I figured out what it was saying."

His entire notebook was filled past the margins. Arrows were drawn chaotically. I stared at it until the pieces fit.

"It says . . . I am family. It is a part of me. A father, or cousin, or sister even," he revealed. "It knows I am alone. It wants to save me."

Jealousy kept me warm at that moment.

"Why have I not heard it? Why have I not seen it again? I love it just as much," I replied. A weakness hit my knees. The homeless man broke my fall with his arms.

"It requires much sacrifice. You must believe," he said. "I will stay with you. We are chosen." He leaned over to peek at the drawings and curled his bottom lip upward. "Although, we are not the same."

I awoke the next day perspiring. The sun was right above me. Nearly everyone around me was wearing shorts, tank tops, and hats. The still water was now a rivulet. When I walked back to my apartment, the key didn't work. The security guard did not recognize me. The street seemed to stretch when I walked back to the park. My mouth was dry, lips cracked. I felt as though I was in an inverted world where instead of me people-watching, the whole world was staring at me. Mocking my commitment, waiting for my testimony. The homeless man was where I'd left him. He handed me a cold can of beans.

"You're back. I've protected our valuables." His eyes darted. "I have a feeling it will return tonight," he whispered as he leaned close to my face. "It came to me. A vision."

I balled my fist and attempted to save face. "Do you have something to write with?"

"Yes." The homeless man handed me a pen with specks of blood on the barrel. "Do not lose it."

I slipped into a dream where the ocean was beneath my feet. I saw someone in the vanishing point. Unable to scream, due to my mouth being sewn shut, I waved my hands. It mimed me, then pointed down. Submerged below was the world I used to know. Cityscapes, commuters, lights, cars, traffic, pigeons, life. A tear lifted from my cheek and floated upwards into an empty black sky. A hand landed on my shoulder. When I turned around, nothing, no one, was there. When I looked forward, nothing, no one, was there. When I looked down, nothing, no one, was there. I was alone.

A kick to my ribs woke me up. The homeless man sprinted to the rail, peering over into the lake. It took some effort to lift my body. Malnourishment was taking its toll.

"Do you see?" he yelled. "It has returned to us!"

I squinted as hard as I could and advanced near him. On the lake, bathed in moonlight, a black swan rested, with two small white chicks at its side.

"There is nothing here," I responded.

The homeless man's pupils dilated, and his mouth remained agape.

"There is nothing here!" I yelled it again, and the homeless man dropped to his knees.

"Take me . . . free me from this place," he began to murmur repeatedly. "I am alone. Alone in a world that does not understand me. That does not understand your love. Free me from this place."

I grabbed his shoulders and began shaking him. "Is it speaking to you? Why can't I see?"

"He is a heretic." The homeless man shook from my grasp. "He is unable to perceive your mercy."

Panicked, I reached in my pocket for the pen.

"He is undeserving. I am your child," the homeless man yelled as I jammed the pen into his neck.

Watching the blood squirt from his puncture wound made me light-headed. It was as if we were dying together. When his body hit the ground, I passed out. When I woke up, I felt pain in my hands. In the center of both my palms was a hole covered in scabs.

I stayed awake for the next few days, eating scraps from the garbage, leering at passersby. The homeless man never returned. Perhaps he had been saved. Or, maybe I killed him? I found solace in my drawings. I started chanting what I last heard the homeless man say: *Take me, free me from this place.*

A sound of crackling leaves emerged from behind. I covered my mouth as a cough escaped. The back of my hand was wrinkled. My arms were stick-thin, and walking became an arduous process. A fresh-faced man appeared, carrying fruit and water. He handed it to me carefully. I went for the water first. Every sip was granting me more life. He sat silent, watching me ravage the fruit, then sat next to me and extended his hand.

"I can bring more," the fresh-faced man said. "There are others who will come as well."

"Others?"

"Yes." He let his gaze rest on the lake. "We need you fed and in good health."

"Thank you."

"Praise be. How long have you been here?"

"Forty-five days. Four hundred and five days. I can't remember."

I watched him scurry off in a hurry. The food began to digest in my stomach and I lifted my old bones. I took a solemn walk around the trail in the park, using a long branch for assistance. Peering into the majestic water of the lake, I searched for old memories. But all I found was hollowness. As if my soul was lost in a bottomless cave. The weather felt strange on my skin. The world had passed through me, leaving behind this shell of a believer. An obsessive. A destitute. I placed the tip of the pen to my neck, pressing it into a vein. The injury inside my palms stopped me from breaching. I touched the sunken parts of my face. Felt my ribs glide on across my fingertips. Mother always said thinkers are in a lifelong pursuit of searching. I'd reached my end. As I stumbled back to my place between the trees, I saw a lit candle surrounded by all my drawings. The moon was full. The streetlight began to pulse. A dragonfly glided on the still water.

"He has returned," the fresh-faced man announced. "The Witness."

A group of strangers got on their knees. Near them were gifts, food, money. Tears in their eyes. A feeling of togetherness amongst them. A blur crossed the starry sky.

"The Witness," they all said together in harmony.

A gust of wind hit the back of my neck. I heard a noise behind me. Slowly, I turned around.

THE SIXTY-FIVE PERCENT

"THE VOLTAGE IS TOO HIGH," Abbot warned as the ceiling above him coughed dust and cracked in several places.

"I'll lower it," Leeto responded, watching the front door absorb repeated kicks, shoulder rushes, and battering rams. "Thirty more seconds."

Leeto watched the shadows of legs sweep across the brick walls. Numerous soldiers were arriving at his underground bunker. Out the small window above a gurney, light from explosions temporarily flashed the carnage the earth was enduring. Amid war, two scientists, one old and one young, managed to subdue an enemy.

A scalpel was used to open the enemy's temple. A spliced coax cable with no outside insulation was connected to the brain. An interface on a monitor displayed the configurations. Abbot held the screen near his chest, wiping his sweat by switching arms, not realizing how heavy the equipment was. Leeto input the code on a keypad protruding from the middle of the cord.

"Fifteen more seconds," Leeto breathed.

The butt of an assault rifle demolished the windows. A cacophony of mutters took place amongst the attackers. Their interaction sounded like the buzzing of flies trapped inside an amplifier, all with different sized wings, traveling at different speeds, and attuned to different frequencies. Once their meeting concluded, a small pipe bomb was thrown inside. Smoke escaped from beneath the door, post-detonation. At its limit, the entrance collapsed.

A battalion penetrated the space. Engulfed in black dust, they switched their POV to night vision. They had ectomorph-shaped bodies with hardened skin—a combination of cobalt and melded tungsten. Visors replaced eyes. They had no necks below their pentagon-shaped helmeted heads. Exaggerated muscle mass was carved on their chest, legs, and arms for aesthetics.

All that was left in the damaged area were spots of blood on the gurney, a broken monitor, a severed cable, and a pair of glasses. The smell of melted plastic overtook any other scents. The attackers didn't have noses, but rather receptors that transcribed smells into colors, and colors into language.

The objects in the room were assaulted with malice by the battalion as it briefly separated from the Hive mind. All the furniture had been overturned. All the cushions had been stabbed. Cases were broken, drawers violently ripped from hinges. Small containers were shot at before being studied and surveyed. Multicolored liquids held in beakers bled into crevices in the ground.

Freely continuing their orgy of destruction, none of the attackers noticed a few loose bricks below their feet.

"It's filthy down here," Abbot complained, hunching his body into the sewer pipe. A rivulet of brown water soaked his socks. Insects of unknown origin slithered above him. He adjusted his lab coat, pulled up his tan pants, and accepted the fact that his oval glasses had a crack at the top.

"We are alive, and we have him." Leeto dragged the unresponsive body of his enemy-experiment. "He is beautiful."

"He is dead."

"No," said Abbot. "There is a disc processing in his brain. In silence, it can be heard. The machine still lives."

"They have brains?"

"More like brain tissue surrounding the artificial frontal lobe."

"Where will this tunnel lead us?" asked Abbot. "No, wait, more importantly, how long until we can be on land?"

"It empties at Avalon, in three miles. It's a Silent Zone. Safe enough."

"Three miles?" Abbot gasped.

"Follow my voice when it becomes too dark to see, and be grateful."

The exit had a dip of about ten feet which Leeto hadn't anticipated. He fell awkwardly on his shoulder, straight into the shallow water but near land. The experiment fell on its back, but the combat vest attached to its ribs protected it from injury. Abbot, being the last one, carefully went out feetfirst to his amusement, and saw the crest of mushroom clouds on the horizon. It'd become a regular sight for him these days, like a pinch of stars on a clear night.

"They say at your age one fall is all it takes," Abbot said as he approached Leeto to help him up. Leeto's lab coat was competely drenched and covered in mud. Abbot thought it represented Leeto's personality: a specialized mess.

"Something like this isn't worthy enough to take me out," Leeto said, wiping leaves off his pants. "We need to find any remains we can. The experiment's metal is heavier than expected."

The place called Avalon held an eerie calm. Neither wildlife nor human life existed, as far as anyone knew. The opposition had decimated everything a decade ago. Given the amount of nuclear interference, many species living in the water were permanently mutated. On land, the surviving humans had migrated.

"I see dead bodies," Abbot said. "No, let me correct myself. Dead *mutated* bodies of what appears to be fish." He took out a small square device with two lenses in the front, similar to a pair of vertical binoculars, and placed it next to his eye. Small fibers protruded and attached themselves around his pupil. In his view, Avalon became a topographical map. The heat sensor in the device couldn't detect a thing. "This technology is fascinating," Abbot declared.

Leeto rubbed his shoulder as they made their way toward the shore. "Everything from Jexa is better than ours. Eras ahead."

Abbot continued to survey. "There's a van. I doubt there's fuel. We can check the tank."

"Let me see." Leeto snatched the device and examined the vehicle through the lens. The doors were riddled with bullet holes. The windshield was shattered and the hood was dented. "Okay, take the experiment; I've marked the destination." He pocketed the device. "I have a kill switch and an interface on my waterproof watch, so you shouldn't have any—"

"No." Abbot cleared his voice after it had squeaked and repeated himself. "I do the recon, and you carry the purse. This is the same thing that happened at Kitt, and at Bragder. I am your colleague, not your working hand. Plus, I'm worried about the details you left out of this mission. This quest of nonsensical means."

To Leeto, Abbot's words were like rain on an empty street, draining into the sewers. Leeto tapped the shoulder he had fallen on. "It's worse than it seems. Put your youth to good use. Grab him by the collar and pull with your knees."

Abbot grumbled curse words under his breath and glowered at Leeto, now noticing his jaundiced eyes. The white whiskers escaping Leeto's ears and nose and knuckles. The saggy skin on his neck. The surprising amount of muscle on his arms. Not to mention the zigzag scar from his eyebrow to his top lip, acquired while saving Abbot's life.

Abbot had been three, but the trauma had set in deep; all the emotions of that day he could recall in an instant. Smokeless green fire surrounded his room. Yelling and pulling and shooting damaged his ears. Leeto's cold hand when he pulled him from his bunk bed and fled the orphanage. No one else survived.

"Fine." Abbot brought himself to the present reluctantly while squatting, trying to figure the best way to drag the unconscious soldier. "When he wakes up and snaps my neck, I want you to cry so loud they hear you all the way in Wils."

"My boy," Leeto said, "there's no one alive in Wils. Not anymore."

"The sentiment is the same."

"Come, come, we're wasting energy."

The van looked better up close. Abbot looked around for a seat. After that long trek, he was exhausted. For lack of a better place he sat on the experiment's chest, sipping synthetic fluids from a waterskin.

Leeto, feeling cautious, scanned the vehicle three times over. A nervous tick formed in his fingers. He began picking at his cuticles. He forced himself to breathe deeply before taking out a small metal square from his pocket. He shook out the sewer water inside, then pressed the center button. It unfolded into the shape of a pistol. The LED screen on the back read: 6x ammunition.

"I thought you were left-handed?" Abbot questioned from a distance, in between sips.

"I am."

"You fell on your left shoulder."

"It's much better now." Leeto readied himself in an

antiquated officer stance with the pistol drawn.

"Of course it is," Abbot said, rolling his eyes. "Call me if you need me. I'll be doing what I always do."

Behind Abbot's ears were two small zippers. As he pulled them down, thin antennae jutted from both. The tips blossomed into a circular design of metal plates that resembled miniature satellites.

"Do it quietly," said Leeto as he crept toward the trunk, noticing it was propped open. He slowly lifted it with the barrel of the gun, expecting a mine trap to detect skin contact. Inside were transport materials used for medical supplies. Hazmat bags filled with a saffron liquid and random body parts: heart, liver, lungs. He closed the trunk and walked to the right side. As he glanced into the back window, he found himself staring directly into the barrel of a submachine gun.

Abbot's satellites were detecting radio waves from the attacker's bases nearby. Anything in a forty-mile radius. Originally encrypted, all the binary language was decoded into tangible speech.

"Insurgents at Kamogelo. Reinforcements required. Control ratio 9 to 1," the dispatcher said over the communication frequency.

Abbot jumped to his feet. "9 to 1?" he whispered to himself.

"Confirmed location. Latitude 38.8951 and longitude 77.0364."

Abbot calculated the coordinates in his head. "Past the mountains."

Leeto raised his hand to show his pistol. He thought the figure holding the submachine gun was an older model attacker. It was programmed with tangible speech and fitted with mock skin to resemble the Original Man. There was a large open wound near his jaw, and as he spoke, Leeto could see the mechanical gears working to make him talk.

"Is this Star Date 4096?" the older model inquired, keeping the gun steady.

"You speak tangibly. Are you a diplomacy droid?" Leeto slowly placed his forehead on the nozzle of the gun. "No . . . you're a nonviolent model from Othelia. Why are you in a Silent Zone?"

The older model readied his position and repeated, "Is this Star Date 4096?" Inside his eyes, several lenses made robotic noises as they scanned Leeto. "You do not have a heartbeat."

"And you, my archaic friend, were not programmed to kill. Unlike me." Leeto blew the older model's head off its shoulders. Sparks flew and wires squirmed from its neck. Oil leaked from every joint as it fell to the ground with a metallic thunk. A small key attached to a globe keychain shifted to the edge of its pocket.

Abbot retracted his satellites at the sound of the gunshot. He stood up, off the unconscious soldier, and peered into the endless space of damaged earth between the trees. He cupped his hands around his mouth to speak but hesitated at the last moment, pondering all the wrong things: Leeto's untimely death. Being lost in enemy territory. The loneliness of surviving war. The never-ending distrust. The lack of the opposite sex. He cupped his hands around his mouth once more, and during his inhale, he heard the sound of a struggling car engine.

The wheels were covered in chains and tore through the grass as Leeto drove the van close to Abbot. Upon opening the passenger door, he tossed Abbot the submachine gun. Unfortunately, the gun pinned him to the ground.

"Keep it. It isn't loaded." Leeto placed the van in park and exited to grab the soldier. "There's plenty of space in the back."

"Is this the gun I heard?"

"No, that was my own." Leeto grunted, pushing the soldier into the back seat, his legs and arms smushed together awkwardly.

"Was someone in the van?" Abbot stood and balanced the weight of the gun so it could be held correctly. There was a red cross on the top of the weapon.

"Warning shot."

"So how do you know this isn't loaded?"

"I checked the clip."

Abbot waved his hand through the air where the clip for the submachine gun would've been. "But there is none."

"Get in the car."

"I found something," Abbot shifted the conversation. "We should go east." From the passenger seat, he pointed toward a long stretch of evergreen forest, which ended with the rise of fault-block mountains.

"Toward Kamogelo," Leeto whispered, driving the van, dodging trees, and tapping the gas gauge where the needle hung lifelessly.

"Yes, I heard over the comms. Control ratio 9 to 1."

"9 to 1? There's that many of us over there? That close to a Silent Zone?" Leeto swerved around a large stone on the road.

"Exactly."

"Why didn't we see any heartbeats?"

"Limitations of the device, I guess," said Abbot indifferently.

"Hmm, it's not ideal. But our original destination, the Sanctuary, is even farther, and that was before this vehicle came into play."

"Do you know that place? Kamogelo?"

Leeto looked in the rearview mirror and saw the unconscious soldier's hand oscillate between an open palm and a closed fist. "I was born there."

"My father was born there too . . . so I'm told." Abbot caressed the handle of the submachine gun.

"Yes, he brought me to you," Leeto replied. "To all the children. However, I could not return the favor."

"When I try to remember his face, I see yours," said Abbot.

"If it helps, you look exactly like him."

After forty minutes, traveling only twenty-five miles, the van gave out. Clouds of black smoke exhaled from the exhaust pipe. All the meters on the dashboard began to go offline one by one, the speedometer erroring out first. As Leeto attempted to pop the hood, a small flame appeared atop the engine. They abandoned the vehicle.

Abbot continued dragging the unconscious soldier.

The sky above them was gradually being swallowed by massive gray clouds. Anytime a thunderstorm appeared, they knew it would be black rain. No one had seen regular rainfall in over fifteen years. Abbot had never seen it in his lifetime, only described in old undamaged texts. Luckily, they noticed the foot of a mountain was within walking range.

They forded a river, Abbot resting his arms on the unconscious soldier who floated due to his vest. Ever vigilant for nearby foes, Abbot unzipped one zipper from behind his ear and let a miniature satellite deploy to search for signals.

"Double-check what you heard earlier. I can't imagine there are many of us here. Unless the attacker's presence is very low," Leeto warned as they reached the center of the stream. "I'll admit, this area is not what I thought it would be. I assumed it to be barren. But there are many things below the surface here. Metaphorically, of course."

"I don't hear anything anymore," said Abbot as he surveyed the area around him. There was artificial silence; something was blocking everything else. He didn't expect any noise from the wildlife. Animals were scarce after the chemical waste from nuclear weaponry had found its way into rivers and lakes. Leeto and Abbot's entire diet consisted of rations that never tasted like the flavor described on the label.

"We'll keep on course, just in case." Leeto sounded tired as they made it to the other side of the stream. "Wish to make camp?"

"I thought we agreed on the mountains." Abbot cleared the way, dragging the soldier along, using a sling to keep the submachine gun on his person.

"Right." Leeto yawned. "How much farther?"

"You took the device, Leeto. Remember?"

Leeto struggled to keep his eyes open. "Ah, yes, yes." He sat and emptied his front pockets onto the grass. Several square metal objects fell out. Each with different symbols and labels. He had even kept the van key. "Where did I put it last?"

"Side pocket."

"Side pocket," said Leeto agreeably as he unclipped the small pouch on his right pants leg and took it out. "This is why the old need the young."

"If I have to drag this dead body any longer, I'm going to age ten years tonight," said Abbot.

"One of those metal squares is a small medical transport droid," Leeto explained. "I imagine the wheels to be too small, of course. Being used for stethoscopes, thermometers, defibrillators, things of that nature. But we can rig it to move the soldier. The living soldier."

"Right, the living soldier who hasn't moved in hours," Abbot said. He stretched his back and noticed the soldier rotate his wrist in a complete circle. He pretended not to see it and continued talking. "Why do they have all that stuff if Jexa is ninety-five percent metal?"

"To keep us alive." Leeto sighed.

"I thought the idea was to keep us dead."

"In the long run, yes. This is more for experimentation. Reverse engineering of the enemy will provide immeasurable results. Same thing we're doing."

"Same thing *you're* doing," said Abbot.

"Always prepared with teenage rebellion, just resting at the tip of the tongue," Leeto sniped.

Abbot began inspecting some of the metal squares, searching for clues from the symbols etched into them. "Of course." He tried the first one he picked up.

A small metal tray unfolded, three wheels sticking out the bottom. Leeto nodded in approval. Abbot looked at the soldier, then back to the tray, then back to the soldier. Leeto inadvertently nodded once more from fatigue. He made an awkward smile as he sprang up from the ground.

"Best do this now. I'm running on fumes." Leeto began to walk deeper into the woods toward the mountains.

"Wish I fell on my shoulder at one hundred and five years old," Abbot grumbled, as he hesitantly propped the soldier on the tray. "You were right, you know. This thing is alive. I saw it move."

"It'll talk eventually." Leeto checked the interface on his watch. "Soon enough."

The base of the mountain they approached was intimidating. The mutation from the damaged earth caused odd-colored vines to spring from below and wrap themselves inside the rock. Following a small animal trail at the base, the two companions were able to find a small opening on one side. Beyond the entrance were small pockets of blackwater, deep enough for them to sleep in, yet with no room to stretch or roll, tall enough to jump into without injury. Abbot left the soldier outside, covered beneath a makeshift bed of leaves for disguise.

"I'm sure there's a yawning nearby. We'll find it in the morning," Leeto suggested, looking up at a full moon.

"A what?"

"A large opening to a cave. This place isn't uncharted. All of this is man-made." Leeto rubbed the cave walls and felt the etching of words carved there. Long sentences of a dead language spiraled up to the ceiling. "Probably before and after the Scarlex War."

Abbot snuggled into his carbon sleeping bag. He placed the submachine gun near his feet. "I read about that." After a change of heart, he put the gun closer, snugged under his arm.

"We ruined all that we built," Leeto said. "Which, in some way, is all man can do in his lifetime. Build, destroy."

Abbot groaned. "I heard there were more women . . . back then."

"More everything." Leeto's fingers traced the etchings, feeling the words, the remnants of the past. "More life. Us and the Originals lived in harmony."

"I regret that. I mean, if we die tomorrow. Or sometime soon. I regret not having more . . . you know."

"The Sanctuary is amply populated. You'll find a mate." Leeto turned to see Abbot's face. "Have you ever . . ."

Abbot tucked his head lower into his sleeping bag. "Two. One was a stolen kiss. The other was an older woman who went on a mission she knew she wouldn't come back from. Told me I reminded her of her son."

"Incestuous. Another stolen kiss?"

"I'm going to sleep."

"You have plenty of time, Abbot. We've been gone six months."

"That's the problem with old people. A year to you is a nap. For me, it's an eternity. From fourteen to fifteen there are a lot of changes. Things I can't even comprehend. On top of being in a war."

"Ah, but it's good to keep love on the brain. My brain was on work, and when it came to love, I pushed it away. Like how a mathematician might scoff at a children's game."

"There's bound to be some ancient hag somewhere in these woods for you, Leeto," Abbot teased. "Running around naked, just waiting for you to—"

A loud snore from Leeto's direction interrupted Abbot's good-natured taunt. He laid his head down on the hard rock ground and watched the soldier repeatedly open his palm and then make a fist. After the tenth one, Abbot found himself drifting off to sleep.

Abbot woke to find the tip of an obsidian spear inches from his nose. Panicked, he tried to back up and hit the cave wall, the weapon pressing into his skin. Outside, in the black rain, Leeto was lying facedown, bound at the wrists and legs, yelling at a man covered in a black latex suit. They wore gas masks. Its thick goggles disguised their eyes .

Abbot looked around. Based on his internal chronometer, it was still night. He had slept for a mere three hours. The slight movement of his head caused Abbot's attacker to jab his spear tip into Abbot's neck. Clearly, he was not supposed to move.

"Don't touch him!" Leeto screamed.

"*Hkznot sttiung*," said another of the men wearing a latex suit. He raised an ax made of obsidian and began hacking at the unconscious soldier's neck.

"Quiet," another man demanded from a distance, approaching with a radar device in his hand. There were two silver stars on the right shoulder of his suit. Though his face was covered, a powerful aura exuded from him.

His posture gave the impression he found submission akin to death and he spoke again: "The Jexa must be destroyed."

"I've compromised him! He doesn't respond to the Hive mind. I plan to reconfigure him!" Leeto begged as the man continued to bring down the ax with full force, chipping away at the exoskeleton.

"The one in the hole. What is he?" The commander with the silver stars walked past Leeto, pointing at the ground. "If he's sixty-five percent, bring him to me."

"*Wertiuz Holjnis.*" The man with the spear lifted his goggles. A red scanner illuminated the limestone cave walls before washing over Abbot's form. "He's sixty. What enhancements are inside you?"

Abbot lifted his hands to forestall any threats, carefully maneuvering himself from the sleeping bag, keeping the submachine gun hidden beneath it. The spearman lowered his weapon. Abbot revealed the zippers behind his ears.

"Bring him unharmed," the commander ordered. He watched the axman steadily attempting to cause damage to the unconscious soldier. Despite his efforts, he'd only made a three-inch mark.

"They've advanced again. What of this one?" He pointed to Leeto.

"The scans were inconclusive, Scyther. He shows one percent. He is something else." The spearman allowed Abbot to move toward the cave exit.

"Lift him from the ground." Scyther, the commander, took the radar device and waved it over Leeto's body. After the scan, he opened his palm to the axman. The axman nodded and handed Scyther the weapon. "Remove his shirt," he ordered.

Leeto resisted as his shirt was torn away, exposing large scars, wounds from lacerations, and staples on his side. He peered at Abbot, mouthing the words: *do not look.* Scyther tapped the edge of the ax on Leeto's bare chest. He sniffed Leeto's hair and examined his left shoulder. There was a red blemish, but no sign of blood.

Abbot couldn't bear to see Leeto cut to pieces. "I vouch for him! He is the same! Like me!" Abbot pleaded.

"He must say many things." Scyther leaned back and slammed the ax into Leeto's chest as hard as he could, the handle shaking in his hand. He pulled the blade out, torn pieces of synthetic skin sticking to it. Metal showed in the gash. "He is worse than Jexa."

Abbot gaped at his companion in disbelief. He'd never seen Leeto bleed from an injury. Nor had he seen Leeto age in his fifteen years of life. Black rain danced on the edge of the blade as Scyther prepared for a second swing. He was smiling beneath his mask, swelling with pride and malice. "He'll break easily."

At that moment, the no-longer unconscious soldier lifted himself from the ground. A series of clacking noises erupted from his stomach. With one palm open, he summoned the hidden submachine gun magnetically. Abbot's sleeping bag was also caught in his grip and he was yanked forward out of the speartip's range.

The soldier turned the gun on the axman and shot twice, hitting him in the neck. As the axman collapsed, the soldier pointed at Scyther. There was only a *click-click* as the trigger was pulled. The other man in a latex suit took notice and pointed his gun in the soldier's direction. A powerful bass sound emitted from inside Leeto's body.

"I can make him stop!" Leeto screamed without moving his mouth. "No one else has to die."

Scyther lowered his ax and slowly backed away, signaling to his partner to do the same. "Make it so," he said calmly.

The no-longer unconscious soldier powered down and his shoulders slouched forward. The submachine gun dropped into the damp grass. Abbot focused on catching his breath, staring at the corpse, following the blood streaming into the dirt. Leeto sat up and buttoned his shirt with his usual dignity before unsheathing his pistol. He'd heard of the men in black latex suits.

"How many are you?" Leeto inquired, pistol now drawn.

"I should ask you the same," Scyther responded.

"You're the only one who knows the modern language? I've heard your men. They haven't been taught."

"The ways of the sixty-five percent? No. I prefer them untainted."

Leeto paused, expecting Abbot to speak. In his silence, he pressed on for more information.

"The communication over the airwaves. You're making a honeypot."

The ground shook beneath them. Heavy artillery, something mobile, was approaching the vicinity. Faint sounds of helicopters could be heard. Scyther turned his head to Abbot but sent his question to Leeto.

"Can he see as well as you?"

"He will follow my voice," Leeto answered.

"Does he know why he follows you at all?"

"Jexa are approaching," Abbot interrupted, wide-eyed, with his satellites out from behind his ears.

"I promise the boy no harm." Scyther flipped a switch on the back of his suit, near the neck. In seconds, his entire body was camouflaged. A silhouette of him could be seen from the black rain above. His partner did the same, and they began zigzagging through the woods.

The no-longer unconscious soldier stood up. Abbot watched Leeto press seemingly random buttons on his chronometer. When Leeto turned to look at him, Abbot couldn't make eye contact. Instinctively, he shortened the space between them. Emotionally, he was caught between heartbreak and confusion. Leeto attempted to reach out with his hand, but feeling Abbot's reluctance, he pulled it back.

"All can be explained," Leeto whispered as he began following the camouflaged men.

"This entire time? Were you leading me to betrayal?" Abbot's voice squeaked, and he did not attempt to deepen it.

"I was sent to kill you long ago, but your father—" Leeto stopped when the sounds of vehicles rose. "I would never hurt you. For now, we must be sharp. They know the ways of earth better than we do."

"How so?"

"They are the Original Man."

The underground base was elaborate. Leeto assumed it must've taken at least a hundred years to design and build. All its limestone walls were covered in the dead language. Pockets of light came from rows of torches resting in sconces. Huge vents covered in moss opened and closed, releasing steam through a central opening above. Abbot saw the Original Men's faces, with tribal paintings under their eyes bearing red and yellow markings. He saw families huddled in cubbies, glancing at him and pointing at Leeto.

Scyther took off his mask when they arrived at the main console. He was dark-skinned with no tribal markings at all. His eyes were low, his jaw square. On one of the monitors was a large spherical object made of eggshell hexagon plates. It was sitting on a stand made of steel, eight poles covered in gold protruding with bulbs at their tips pulsating blue light.

"I have your word that nothing will happen to my, uh, experiment," Leeto said, gesturing toward the conscious soldier who was placed in a secluded facility in the base.

"I have its controller right here." Scyther tapped Leeto's left shoulder. "Best not to frighten the people. We are fragile. We can't even walk outside without protective gear because of what the nukes have done to the atmosphere. The man your experiment killed had no next of kin. His death ends his lineage."

"I'm sorry. I won't tell anyone." Leeto held out a hand, offering a truce.

"Does the boy know we exist?" Scyther moved a joystick on the main console to zoom in on the spherical object. "That the sixty-five percent are not the heroes? That he is more human than they are?"

"He knows what I tell him," Leeto answered.

Scyther glanced down at Abbot. He could sense him shrinking, wanting to disappear. Not knowing his worth or origin. He was being subdued into a blank state. Scyther paused and went back to the monitors. "I'll leave that to you."

A few of Scyther's men rushed toward him. They stopped in unison and bowed. The tallest one walked forward from the middle and kneeled.

"*Weinkju Hak*," he said.

"Twenty minutes," Abbot repeated, having decoded the man's speech. "What does that mean?"

Scyther, with a cheerfully surprised look, answered him. "We're going to detonate it."

"Another nuke?" Leeto asked.

"Not quite."

On the outdoor security camera, a strange entity was floating in the sky above the trees. Its presence was ominous and oddly peaceful, like an infant moon making its way to the stratosphere. Scyther zoomed in on it. "This is new."

It looked like an orange orb surrounded by three silicon appendages, one in the front, two on the sides. Massive in scale, it was hovering thirty feet in the air. The design resembled Jexa armor.

"They advance faster than we can catch," Scyther claimed.

A bomb hit. The shock rattled the cave walls. A few screams could be heard. Scyther's men came running up the stairs toward him as the ceiling collapsed. Chunks of heavy limestone and steel support poles and barriers crushed them instantly. Alarms blared and backup generators sprung on. Defensive shields rose from an armory below and deployed themselves over the hole rent by the bomb.

"I thought you said we had twenty minutes?" Abbot screamed as the pandemonium continued.

Missiles began hitting the sides of the base but weren't able to penetrate. Scyther put his black latex suit back on.

"*Zarilah!*" Scyther yelled to a panel above, where members of his team were scrambling on a large computer to check surveillance and damage to the base. "What happened to the intel?"

Above, holding onto the rail one-handed in case another bomb went off, Zarilah typed furiously on the keyboard, scanning for viruses and software errors. "Once Jexa got within fifty miles of the vicinity, they bugged our system. The twenty-minute ETA wasn't from them. It was from the sixty-five percent. Their squadron is headed here."

"Honeypots catch all things," Leeto interjected.

"We wanted the sixty-five to come first." Scyther looked back at the main console. On the security camera, the floating entity was gone. "We need to detonate it now."

"It'll kill us," Leeto warned.

"It will kill *you*. I can place a shield around the boy. That Jexa ragdoll deserves to die."

"A shield?"

"It's a nuclear electromagnetic pulse big enough to spread across whole states, even oceans. It's our chance to stop both of you."

"I didn't want this to happen." Leeto rolled back his sleeve. His hand began to move inhumanly, then mechanically shifted inside his forearm. A Gatling gun protruded out. "You have to let us escape before you do this."

"You won't be able to outrun it."

"Then give me three shields."

Another bomb rattled the ceiling, putting dents in the shields. All the screaming stopped when the floating entity descended inside the base. It had a translucent yellow trail behind it. Up close, the sight was divine. No one had ever seen such a Jexa machine. It rotated slowly as the appendages spread out.

A few of Scyther's men began shooting at it with machine guns. Every bullet was absorbed. Seconds later, it rocketed through a giant wall in the base, arriving at the nuclear electromagnetic pulse. The front of the entity began to alter, forming an opening. Power suction could be heard as it began pulling the nuclear electromagnetic pulse into itself.

"I'm doing it now!" Scyther leaned forward on the control panel and lifted the button cover. Right as his fist was inches from the button, Leeto struck him hard in the back of the head. Abbot watched him fall, out cold.

"Why would you do that?" Abbot, shaken with fear, tugged on Leeto's lab coat.

"It would kill us all," Leeto responded, dragging Scyther from the console as more missiles continued to hit the base.

"He said I was more human."

"You are, but the side effects are unknown."

Meanwhile, the entity managed to swallow the nuclear electromagnetic pulse wholly. It detonated inside, causing it to implode. Once it had completed, the entity had shrunk to the size of a small mangled ball of shrapnel and dropped to the ground.

Jexa troops began descending into the base, firing at will. Leeto released the powerful bass sound from within, took Abbot's hand, and begin searching for an escape from the chaos.

"I know Jexa tactics. They'll flank left first," Leeto said, as they dodged the gunfire exchange nearby. "The soldier is paired to me now. He will follow to where we are."

"Are you controlling it from within? Is the chronometer a façade?"

"In this case you are correct."

Helicopters swarmed above the gaping holes the base had endured from the earlier attacks. Armed with an artillery of their own, bearing a black flag symbol of three stripes on the sides, the sixty-five percent squadron began attacking the Jexa troops. From a loudspeaker, everyone could hear the voice of the squad leader.

"Hide in all corners and safe areas of your base. We will not fire upon you. Do not venture outside, for the area is filled with warfare. I repeat . . ." the squad leader announced.

"Do not heed this advice," cried Leeto. "Everything is going on inside. Outside there is a way to safety." He located a small gate at the bottom of a wall near the moss-covered vents. "Are you harmed in any way?"

Abbot didn't respond. Leeto kicked at the gate, making a hole. He crouched down and began to crawl into it. Abbot stood, holding back tears, watching the now-conscious soldier catch up to them.

"Tell me the truth," Abbot demanded.

"Now?"

"Yes. Right now. I don't care if I die."

"You don't know what you're saying; your emotions—" Leeto's sentence was interrupted as the fighting inside took on new life.

More bodies of all kinds were taking their last breath—Jexa, the Original Man, and the sixty-five percent alike.

"Abbot, please!" Leeto pleaded. "I'm still the same person you know."

"I don't know who you are!"

Leeto, growing impatient, picked up Abbot by the waist and pushed and kicked him through the small gate's hole, onto the path that ended at the foot of the fault mountains. Numerous spotlights were shining on the ground. Leeto, putting Abbot in a fireman's carry, avoided all the attention, racing for pastures that led to hills and valleys.

After thirty minutes of running, Leeto managed to find a safe space near a waterfall. The three crowded together by the rapids. The now-conscious soldier mimicked Leeto's movement: when Leeto sat, he sat. Abbot turned his back to both of them, staring silently into the approaching sunrise.

"Does the sanctuary exist?" Abbot questioned.

"No answer I can say right now will suffice." Leeto kept them moving until the battle sounds from the base quieted. "When you're ready, we'll press on."

Abbot suddenly perked up, his ear-satellites protruding. "I hear someone."

A few bushes shook in the distance, and a slender leg came out. It was another Original Man in a black latex suit, but the shape was much different than the others. It was dragging a colleague by the collar through the dirt. A trail of blood coursed from his lower back.

Leeto freed the Gatling gun from his forearm.

"No." Abbot pushed Leeto's arm down.

"Please, we . . . we abandoned our station." The slender intruder coughed, pressing a button on her goggles. It transitioned the dark shade to clear glass.

Abbot froze, a pair of jade eyes staring back at him.

"Do you have painkillers?" the female inquired.

The other Original Man on the floor was breathing heavily. He rolled over to expose a gash across his back. Struggling, he crawled toward the slender one's boot and stuck his hand inside. He pulled out an obsidian blade.

"Stop! You shouldn't be moving," the woman said and bent down to stop him.

The Original Man moved away from her advance and took off his mask, breathing in the deadly carcinogens from the air. It was Scyther, with the blade tip digging into the skin of his neck. Before he could complete the sweep, Abbot kicked his hand. The blade flew through the air and struck where the black rain pooled in the grass. Tears escaped his eyes, and he hid his face in the wet earth. The woman covered his back.

"It's okay, it's okay," the woman, whose name was Zarilah, soothed him like a child, rocking him in place.

Leeto retracted his weapon. He took a deep breath. "Come with us."

"The places you want to go, they won't allow us." Zarilah didn't look at them when she said it. "We've betrayed our kind. We took an escape route. I forced

Scyther to come along. If he wasn't injured, he never would've—"

"Get your Jexa to kill me." Scyther's voice was full of pain. "Make it so."

"Negative. We'll take both of you," said Leeto. "There are biodomes and safe areas. You can walk freely without protective gear." He sat down and took the small metal objects from his pockets.

"I know which one," Abbot said and pressed on the medical tray they had used before to transport the soldier. He inspected the drawers beneath it. An assortment of medical supplies was inside. He spread them on the ground. "Take what you need."

Scyther kept his face in the dirt.

"It's a bit of a stretch, but with Abbot's communications, we should be able to arrive safely by nightfall," Leeto said. "At worst, tomorrow morning. The sixty-five percent will not persecute you. More than likely, they will want to learn of your ways. Life before enhancements. Before a shorter life span. A human experience."

Zarilah sifted through the supplies, taking bottles, needles, thread, and gauze. Then, in gratitude, she stopped and lightly grabbed Abbot's hands, placing them between her own, and bowed.

"We can save him," she counseled.

Abbot's forehead began to sweat, and he felt an overwhelming desire to urinate. The now-conscious soldier stared at Zarilah performing healing techniques on Scyther, its head tilted to the side. It began documenting, taking video, and scanning through their skin to see if there was internal damage. Childlike, it sat crossed-legged and continued to watch.

"It moved on its own," Abbot murmured to Leeto.

Leeto slyly tapped the side of his head. "I'm teaching it. In case you drag me into the woods one day and need assistance."

Abbot put his hand on Leeto's chest, searching for the place where Scyther's ax had punctured him. "You have . . . organs?"

"Only two."

"And you were sent to kill me?"

"Yes. All of the children. All of the sixty-five percent."

"Tell me again why you didn't."

"Your father was a brilliant man. He captured me. Reverse engineered me. Taught me. He was as much my father as yours."

"And he's dead?"

"I don't know. But this is his will. To save you. His mission was for me to do what he had done. Make Jexa part of us."

Abbot hugged him hard, burying his face into Leeto's chest. Over his shoulder, Leeto could see the soldier gently raising his hand, and Zarilah, reluctantly, placing medical supplies in his palm to hold, while she continued her sutra. Sunlight washed over them. Abbot eventually broke the hug and stared at Leeto's face, focusing on the zigzag scar from his eyebrow to his top lip. Now deeply understanding that everything he'd ever known was a lie.

DEMON ROAD

I LIVED IN A CASTLE MADE OF MUD.
Solid and small enough to make me feel caged. Light
barely escaped the warped brown walls. The house had
had so many ancestors pass away that layers of its spirit
fought each other seasonally. I was doomed.

I believe it was late autumn when my stomach's emptiness
corresponded with my heart. After fifty-five days in solitude,
the hunger monster devoured me. Food had to be acquired.

There used to be another person here to handle
these things during the summer. However, the sunlight

had tempted Kali to search for buried treasure in the cityscape. She thought there were buildings, roads, and regular life beyond the mountains, past the desert plain. All sorts of things underneath the dome. Years ago, I had located the area map before Kali did and destroyed it. I thought it would keep her from leaving me. But I had still woke up one day to find myself alone.

I thought about her wandering hopelessly every night. Helped me sleep.

The gun seemed to have gained ten pounds since the last time I held it. Back when I had protein and enough strength to keep my eyes open. Demon Road. That was my conflict. It was a strip of concrete that resembled a face. The potholes and cracks, eyes and mouth, even teeth. To see it was to survive the trek. To get supplies. To live. I flirted with unlocking the door. Flipped the middle of the knob horizontally, then stepped back a few feet. I knew sunset would be approaching. I needed rest. I thought of Kali. My eyes closed.

A dream crawled into bed with me. Any year before this one blended into an amalgam of forget-me-nots. Trauma was a thick coat I wore at all times. In the dream memory, my father lashed at the front door with a hammer, yelling and drinking. A woman covered my eyes halfway during the process. Her hand was rough and smelled of sage. All I could hear was something being dragged. When I was allowed to see again, there was a small wooden table in a room covered with one hundred lit candles.

"They're attracted to natural light," my father said as he tapped a dead light bulb suspended above us. "At least until fall, when the man in the clouds will make it dark for us."

"Then, eventually, no light at all," the woman added, stabbing on her plate what I assumed was some part of a pig.

I climbed the chair to get to my plate on the table. There were greens on one side, a slab of unknown meat on the other. All of it repulsed me. I grabbed a small knife by its wooden handle. There were names carved in it, but since I could not read, the shapes and etchings meant nothing to me. Prisoners weren't allowed outside knowledge. My father shifted in his seat, wiping dribble from the corner of his mouth.

"We eat and kill with the same tools." He swallowed. "If need be. If—"

"Let the boy live as a boy," the woman interjected.

"Where's Grandpa?" I asked innocently, in a voice long dead to me now.

There was a brief pause sprinkled with several looks, sighs, burps, some stretching.

"He's gone out to find Demon Road," the woman finally answered. "We mustn't follow."

"He didn't like it here no more?" I questioned, poking at my food with the small knife.

"He didn't want to live anymore," my father said. "It's hard to exist trapped inside a house for decades."

The daylight pierced my eyes. I had a crust built up in the corners from dried tears. I placed a pot of coffee on the stove and looked at all the melted candles that used to live here. I felt the same way, an extinguished light inside an odd shape. Grandpa didn't want to live anymore. So he went outside. I hadn't showered since Kali left. I hadn't been able to smell for three months.

Someone above must be laughing at me. The man in the clouds. I laughed back and the echo frightened me. I drank the sugarless coffee while it was piping hot and edged toward a crack in the wooden planks nailed to the wall, an ersatz window. Within those few centimeters, I watched the door to the house across Demon Road from me open slowly. The creak of the hinges resembled an animal's cry.

There were rules. A gangly adolescent stepped into the world covered head to toe, wearing huge goggles over his eyes. I saw knives on his belt. A hand cannon held close to his face. Rule one: *The earlier the better*. Father was wrong about a lot of things. It wasn't the sunlight that attracted them. It was us.

Rule two: *Travel in twos at a minimum*. Another teen emerged. Same equipment, same stance, more than likely the same family. They stalked parallel to each other and had crossed a small amount of space before one of them spotted it.

Rule three: *If you see it, kill it.* I watched their inexperience. I watched their bullets miss. I watched them retreat. One tripped. The other abandoned his flesh and blood. At seven feet, they encountered a baby one. Thirty years old, maybe younger. Its heart was beating outside its flesh, covered in purple vines that proved difficult to penetrate. Their skin was verdant-colored, scaled, undulating. Three eyes going horizontally across an oblong skull. Two holes on each cheek that worked as nostrils. Technically, this was their home. We were the invaders.

The gangly one ran inside his house and closed the door. The other had got his leg caught in the predator's hands. Its nails sank into his thigh and outstretched branches traveled up inside him, escaping the top of his head in a burst that caused blood to rain. The thing dropped to the ground when the attack was done and let out one last breath. Crimson-colored grass began to grow over both of them.

Rule four: *A life for a life.* Once it killed, it died.

I had patches of crimson grass in my backyard sprouting into small trees with warped twigs like strands of DNA. At times, strange fruit blossomed from them. It was a slow process. Whenever I became moody, I noticed it more. I obsessed over the size and shape. Then, I shot them from a distance with my pistol before they could bloom. I watched them squirm and ooze and pulsate and cease to move. I made a game out of it.

To show solidarity, I lit a candle and displayed it so my neighbor could see it. He didn't respond with a candle of his own. He wanted to be left alone in the darkness for a while. I kept the flame alive as long as I could. A poor man's vigil.

Another day passed. I made no progress. The shadows in my room were growing taller than me, thriving off paranoia. Life was supposed to be different, they said. A new world, they preached. And as I lay thus sermonized, I realized the choice was never mine to make. I was a casualty of past decisions. Sins of the father, and his father, and his father . . . Like everyone. I promised myself I'd venture out the next day.

Day three. Daybreak. The air tasted metallic and my left eye twitched uncontrollably. Old proverbs from my mother ran through my head unencumbered. I knew the way but never went. Fantasized about it in early childhood. At the end of Demon Road was a dome run by humans. Agriculture and a barter system inside. Enough to sustain for a few months. Rumors of a city made of gold behind it. Fables galore. A door opened. Not my own. I closed mine behind me.

The gangly child reappeared. He wore goggles stained with regret, but I could tell his eyes were sharp. We prepared for round two, our acknowledgment a mutual raising of firearms. A part of me died when I stepped off my porch. We stalked in parallel. Just like before.

Rule five: *If one doesn't make the journey, bring back rations for the fallen's family.* I spoke through the gray mask covering my mouth.

"I am Malachi of the Ruin family. The last standing." My voice broke several times throughout the introduction. I hadn't spoken in some time. Even when Kali was around, we would go silent for weeks.

"I am Caleb of the Settler family," he said, looking above me as if the sky would provide him answers. "Last standing."

"I have lost my map." I said the words sluggishly in my lie. "But I remember the way to Elysian."

Caleb opened his duffle bag and took out a tattered map, offered it to me. "In case we get lost."

Carefully we began traversing the rain-shadowed desert. The land had been forced into this hazardous terrain because mountain ranges blocked all plant-growing and rainy weather. Any type of vegetation came from the death of . . .

"So, what did your family call 'em?" Caleb asked, slowing down his pace due to the uneven topography.

"Natives."

"Fair enough."

We passed a stretch of ocotillos in silence. Nearby was a palo verde tree with bright yellow leaves and green stems. The similarities to the earth's atmosphere were this planet's main attraction. So close to home. So much longer to thrive. I studied it for strange fruit. None on any branch. Though the sight was beautiful, it was beginning to bother us. The infinite stretch of purple sand and high dunes. The two suns hovering above, contributing to the aridity. I could see Caleb shifting his head to talk, then killing his sentence, focusing on the path.

"You migrated here about seventy years ago? I remember stories of 'the man on the roof' across the street," I asked, searching for some truth from my father's stories.

"My granduncle. One of the first exiled families. Shot down five . . natives while standing on the roof."

"Story goes that the roof caved in."

Caleb cracked his knuckles. "It did. One got inside. Never came out. That patch of red grass won't leave either. The names of the fallen are here forever." Caleb stared ahead briefly, then continued. "Running out of space."

"Because of yesterday?"

"Yea."

"Brother or father?"

"Sister."

We stopped forty-five minutes into the trek to sip water. Not shared; we each had our own. No one was sure how a person might be infected. Still no natives in sight. An orange prickly pear cactus bloomed suddenly before our eyes, giving us both a shock.

"They're supposed to be on the other side of the mountain range. Breeding season. We can sneak by," Caleb said as he put the cap on his waterskin. "We ran into a stray. Probably a child."

"You trust the seasons?" I said skeptically. "They want us dead. Whether they get us, or we get each other, or we starve to death. Any means. They killed the forgotten people, way off in the desert. A creative type of hell."

"They want us to pay for what our families did."

"That's an antiquated way of thinking," I said. "What do I have to do with my family?"

"Everything."

"I couldn't disagree more," I said, folding my arms.

"If a thief has ten children. Odds are . . ."

"That one of them will be a merchant," I finished. I knew the old saying.

"We think differently." Caleb took out his hand cannon to check the clip, then put it back in the holster. "Regardless, same goal." He nodded at me.

"When's your sentence over?" I smirked as I said it, but he couldn't see my grin behind the mask.

Caleb put his head down. "Ten years from today."

"At least you know. Must be nice."

I began noticing strange things that made me think about how great was our distance from home. Heading back, we would run the danger of night falling. Plus, the midday sun was in full force: we were approaching the vanishing point, infamous for mirages. I watched one form off the flat rock surface as we reached it. A woman twenty feet tall in a multicolored shawl. Her hair defied gravity. Her hands were inviting me.

I was certain Kali had made it this far. She could stay in Elysian. Her family's sins were forgiven. That's why she abandoned me. Over a year ago I discovered her when I was shooting at the trees in my backyard. Nearly scalped her, a half-naked emancipated woman beneath a nest of unkempt black hair. I never asked about her home. We didn't speak until our teeth clenched after the first time we kissed.

"It's okay," I said at the time, watching her cower back.

"I am grateful for the food." Her voice a whisper. "Real food."

"I don't need this type of compensation."

She stretched her neck, calculating if I was lying or not. Finally, she stood straight up. "I've survived from cooking tree bark"

"You have fire?"

"I did."

"Are you infected?"

"No, when the flame touches the bark it cries. When it stops, I eat it."

"Assuming it's dead."

"What else could it be, when something ceases to cry?"

"Soundless weeping." I hesitated, reeling in the emotional depth of what rested at the top of my brain. "That's why you were in my backyard."

"With the size of the tree you have, we can survive for a month. Tearing it down in small pieces."

"With fire."

Kali looked down and rubbed her chin.

I grabbed one of the candles off a rickety table in my living room. "I have fire."

"Look." Caleb nudged me awake.

We'd taken small shifts where one would nap for no longer than half an hour, then switch. The gravity of the planet put more weight on human bones, ergo more fatigue.

"I found one," he said excitedly.

Several joints popped when I sat up on the jagged rock I slumbered on. I patted my person frantically, feeling relief when my index finger curved inside the trigger loop of my hand cannon. "Where?"

It didn't take long to see. It must've been an older one past its life span. The purple vines covering its heart had withered, and crimson grass was growing over its legs. Except, it had moss—maybe some type of mutation. Its skin was transitioning into a grayish blue.

"This is a bad omen," Caleb warned.

"This is just an outlier. One left by the pack. It's damaged."

"Then where's the pack?"

"Miles away." I stretched and shook my head to get fully awake. "Reproducing. Or . . . maybe in our house, eating our food," I joked.

"We should go back."

Though I couldn't see his eyes because of the goggles, I could smell the fear emanating from his skin.

"Going back, we're liable to get lost in the darkness."

"I'm going back." Caleb began to creep away from me.

"Is the Settler family a group of cowards? If a turncoat has ten sons and one daughter, odds are . . . ?"

Caleb paused, indignation in his stance. "Pretty lousy, I'd say."

"Then give me your supplies. The bag." I raised my hand cannon, pointed it at him, cocked it. "Gun too."

Alone again. The blood I licked from my busted lip tasted like copper. There was a newly forming limp in my step, but I pressed on. Rising in the distance was the top of the majestic dome. Alone, yes, but close.

Caleb had left, taking most of my supplies with him. He allowed me to keep my knife as his foot pressed against my wrist, and his gun shook in my face. But he'd left me alive. Caleb was still a child. A child who had defeated a broken man.

Time became my enemy. Nightfall threatened to reveal itself. As I reached the cliff, I watched a medley of lights shine from Elysian. An ultraviolet rainbow in an alien sky. Oddly, a tear escaped my eye. The result of an old memory forgotten. I reached into my bag, grabbed the last of my materials, the rope and the spike, and prepared to descend down the sheer surface. Firmly hammered into a crevice in the rock, I double-checked my spike, connected the rope, and pushed off to get a decent start.

I tried not to look down. On the side of the mountain, shades began to form in the cracks. Each jump took more energy, caused more pain. My wounded foot became useless, and I pushed off with my good foot for the latter half. When I touched the ground and looked up, above was a vast black sky with three crescent moons. One hundred yards ahead was the beginning of Demon Road. Elysian was reachable.

I limped on for about twenty minutes before I noticed a few shadows had life. They morphed. At first a plain dark mass, now it was forming appendages, height, and distinction. Something was waking up. With the tip of my calloused thumb, I tested the sharpness of my blade. Each flick brought me back to my childhood, climbing the chair to reach my plate. What my father had said about the knife.

I pretended like the horror didn't exist. My feet were painful as I pressed on, finally arriving at Demon Road. I had made it. I could hear the buzz of the electronics from the light display at the dome. I could see the small shops inside. The tomato fields. Prairies full of cattle, pallets of rations. I saw my mind leaving my body. A mirage at night?

I could see large black creatures climbing toward me, up the dome's sides, approaching the top. The Natives. Eventually, all I could see was the pack I told Caleb not to worry about. I brought the knife to my face. Moonlight licked the steel. I was prey in a circle of predators. One reached out and I sliced off eight of its twelve fingers. The scream was deafening, and the knife was covered in blue blood, falling to where blades of crimson grass were beginning to sprout. A sharp blow knocked me to the ground. Pieces of me were being devoured in all places. I kept staring at Elysian. I imagined Kali waiting at the door. I closed my eyes.

Heather, Ludwig, and Nathaniel

LUDWIG

I WAS SURPRISED she'd read the first chapter. My tutor usually found small detours around any narrative of mine. It reminded me of looking at a sheet through a magnifying glass, judging the components that hold it together. Inside my glasses were three strands of hair, dust, and a fingerprint, yet, I blinked away their annoyance and kept going. When I finally finished chapter two, I emailed my document to her. She pulled out a cell phone twice the size of her hand and scrolled with her pinky.

"Do you know what a journeyman is?" the tutor asked slyly, leaving a hum of arrogance in the question.

"A nomad?" I responded, unsure.

"Ah, but you do know what failure is?"

"A worker or sports player who is reliable but not outstanding?"

"No, that's what a journeyman is."

"A lack of success?"

"Something wrong, Mr. Falcon?" she asked with bass in her voice. "Your mind seems to be jumbled up. The result of overstimulation, video games, social media, girls with short Catholic skirts, and, most importantly, your parents."

I raised my hand despite being the only person in the garage during my daily tutoring. "Can I speak frankly, Ms. Cumberbatch?"

"When don't you?" she replied sarcastically.

"What does it take . . . wait, let me rephrase. What would it take for me to never see you again?"

She took the blow in stride, as I knew she would. After rotating her shoulders and cracking her knuckles by flexing her fingers, she leaned toward me. "Bad weather."

It rained every day for the next three months. I wanted to comment on the strangeness of my luck in the living room of my house, but my father was mesmerized by the television. In the absence of my uncannily brilliant, breadwinning, late-night-snacking, silently weeping mother, he returned his gaze to the flexible women dancing to music in yoga pants.

I questioned the blood type we share between us daily. Especially when I studied his face. He had big dreamy eyes, contrasted by dark circles from a life's worth of work. There was always gray stubble on his chin, no matter if he went to the barber or not. I always teased that he had the body of a man who worked out in his twenties and gave it up in his thirties.

When a TV commercial portraying hamsters driving a minivan broke his concentration, I opened my mouth to speak. However, it was halted when my Miniature Pinscher awoke from a deep sleep, launched off the couch, and went into what I call a barking tirade.

"Woke up on the wrong side of the Milk-Bone, Sparky?" my dad said, laughing at his own joke.

"His name is Nathaniel, yet you magically seem to always forget that," I quipped.

"Your mother named him that. That's a stupid name for a dog. It's a human name. Nathaniel."

"But it's also your name. Do you think—just hypothetically—that maybe Mom is trying to tell you something?"

"Dog's need dog names. Like Sparky, Lucky, Quirky, et cetera."

"Do all dog names end in 'y'?" I asked.

"According to the dog rules. Yes. Yes, they do."

"What about Chief? That's a dog name."

"Shut up, Ludwig. The show's back on."

I stood up, stepped over the dog, and walked back to my chamber of solitude, which I call my room. "Crazy weather we're having, huh, Nathaniel?" I said under my breath, but he heard me anyway.

"That kooky woman thinks I'm a dog, huh? Well, bark bark, or whatever noise dogs make. And it's Dad to you! Not Nathaniel!" he mumbled to himself.

I closed the door to my room and stared at the twist lock. Every day I stared at it, knowing I could never use it. It took me years to curate my space. Particular posters in particular places, all related to quantum physics, ancient art, and time travel. My gaming chair was the Workinglab Beta 5000. Three vertical monitors, all twenty-seven inches, attached to my custom-built laptop with over a terabyte of space, extreme processing power, and of course, random LEDs to mimic an alien disco.

I had over three thousand friends on social media. My own platform to stream my favorite games I had mastered, and four semi-attractive girls my age who had a crush on me. One, aptly named Angel, had a buzz cut of blonde hair, a tattoo of a tiger near her crotch, and the fiercest eyes I'd ever seen on a human. Yet I only liked the way she looked, not how she acted. Every man's dilemma.

Also, I had two best friends who, between them, had enough dirt on me to blackmail and destroy any political ambition I pondered undertaking. Serious dirt, like the time I peed my pants in biology class, or when I accidentally used the wrong thermometer in the wrong place. To this day I've never been depressed or psychotic or had a nervous breakdown. Ironically, by my parents I felt loved. Despite it all, I had one major problem. Within the boundaries of my own soul, and the complexity of my instincts, I held the burning desire to escape my world. By escape, I mean—

A message appeared on my laptop from Ace-in-the-scroll: What base is breasts again?

I messaged back: Pretty sure it's second. If nipples, second and a half. One nipple, second and one-fourth.

Ace-in-the-scroll replied: Can I call you? Don't want Big Brother to think I'm a pervert.

Fine, but all fourteen-year-olds are perverts, I wrote back, by our nature. I'd be worried if you weren't.

My favorite anime theme blared from my phone. I picked it up after the second ring, waiting for the melody to drop.

"Dude." Ace answered the same way every time he called.

"Ace, how goes it?"

"On the side of the vending machine next to the abandoned arcade, I became a man."

"One-fourth of a man," I responded.

"I wouldn't expect a child to understand," he said, sounding smug.

"Technically, I'm an adolescent. Did you see the Ghost of Danesbury near the creek?" I asked. "I haven't since . . . that time."

"No, but I looked. You logging in? I got, like, fifty kids waiting for me on the server. One of them keeps screaming about Wuhan."

"It'll blow over by tomorrow," I said. "But yea, give me a minute."

"A minute as in, let me check the NSFW subreddits? Or an actual sixty seconds?"

"I'm checking train schedules for March. I think the K and F line will work for the first part."

"Sorry to burst your fanatical bubble," Ace said, "but I bet Pete—not the weird Pete, the regular Pete—twenty bucks that you wouldn't do it. Because I know you. I know the real you. The Nathaniel junior you. The 'cried when big Sheila stepped on your toes' you. Three hours, tops."

"I'm serious, Ace. February 29th. Don't come looking if you don't believe me."

"Please." The line crackled slightly as Ace sighed. "Spare me the theatrics. Look, we've all thought about it. But no one actually does it."

"Except me. I'm the anomaly. I'm actually going to run away. For good."

"The real anomaly is that I played *Brothers in Arms* for two hours without being called a racial slur."

"That too," I agreed. "They always seem to know we're black over the microphone."

NATHANIEL

The day brings nothing new, and the night sweeps me into a drunken chasm I've memorized every corner of. I'm comfortable in the darkness. I'm fully aware that I'm virtuoso at playing "The Fool." Life is more comfortable this way. The less they think you know, the less they'll ask of you. Nobody knows me but me.

I sat in my chair, my favorite chair where my buttocks have created a distinctive groove. I stared at the mindless screen while the plot grew and grew in my head. I couldn't wait to write it down. Until the dog broke my concentration by barking his head off. *Say something stupid*, I thought to myself. *Keep playing that role.*

"Woke up on the wrong side of the milk bone, Sparky?" I blurted out, fully aware my genius son will make a rebuttal immediately.

He droned on about names. I responded with more nonsense. He hit me with the fact that my name matches the dog's. My wife's sick joke at making me feel bad. I complain every chance I get. However, deep down, I don't care at all. This is when she calls me. When she knows I'm thinking about her. She's telepathic but always downplays it, calling it women's intuition.

"Took you that long to answer the phone?" my wife said, in a tone that implied I missed something. "I could've been dead by now."

"It was five rings. What is it? I'm about to go to my study," I said back.

"Can you defrost the steak, check on Ludwig, and make sure the thermostat is working? Because every morning it says ninety, but it feels like seventy-seven. Also, Rebecca is coming over next Thursday. We got the Wilsons on Saturday. And there's that other problem . . ."

"Want me to write all this down?" I asked, feeling irritable.

"You need to with that 'I smoked too much grass in college to remember anything I say' brain of yours," my wife scolded. "Either that or you just don't listen. In fact, I know you don't listen. I know, right now, there's a pile of garbage sitting by the door."

I stretched my neck to look. *Right again, dear—you've won the day.*

"If you did just one of the things I asked of you, within a few days, I wouldn't have to remind you like this," my wife said, launching into one of her favorite lectures. "Your mind just wanders to a place where I don't exist. And I don't like it, Nate. I don't. If you think hard enough, you'll see how this is all connected. You'll see why we have this new problem now," my wife explained.

She always talked fast when she was mad because the issues had built up, like a dam with a small hole turning into a crater. However, once the force of pressure had been released, if memory served, she'd go back to being her usual self.

"So . . . I had that dream again," she confessed. "About the Ghost of Danesbury. She's been talking to me. We were the same age. It could've been me."

"Except you know how to swim," I reminded her.

"She was killed; everyone knows that. You're the only one—"

"It's a fairy tale, to scare children," I interjected. "I know you still believe all that shit, but none of it's real. It's nice to think about, but you're obsessed."

There was silence on the end of the line for a second, then, "'Bye, Nathaniel."

"What?"

With a shrug of my shoulders, I moseyed on toward my sanctuary—my study. My computer was old, with a big CRT monitor that's probably giving me radiation poisoning every night. I heard the loud fans while it was booting, kicking out the dust I never cleaned.

There was a jitter in my fingertips when I finally opened the Word document. I stared at my gorgeous words, all edited, placed within the proper margins. I scrolled to the top to reread my working title: "Enigma Space Corp."

I picked up the phone to call Chance, my brother. There were questions I needed to ask, plot points I needed to orate. He picked up in three seconds.

"Younger One, how art thou?" I asked.

"You on chapter three yet? I'm on nine. Catch up."

"Family keeps me busy."

He laughed in a sinister way. I felt a little embarrassed at using that excuse.

"I'm going to be on five before the night's out."

"Well, don't rush it. Remember the code."

I released a big sigh. "Sci-fi fan fiction is felt, not rushed. Explored, not finite. Created, not written. Allow space to come to you," I said with pure confidence, like a psalm on the lips of a priest.

"So what's up? Stuck on a plot point?"

"Yea," I admitted. "I have the captain finally reaching the caves, but I don't know whether to kill him or have him discover paintings on the wall."

"It's pretty clear, Older One."

"Paintings."

"Of course," my brother answered. "They can be ancient aliens, with early prototypes of pyramids they gave to the Egyptians. It all fits. Except by now they've advanced to floating labyrinths that hover over the enslaved ones who hate the oligarchy and will one day rise to conquer it."

"When I say I love you, just know. On Mom's dead soul, I don't mean it." I laughed, picking up my handle of vodka resting beneath my desk.

"If you were any more dead to me, I'd have to cross the river Styx just to kill you again," he jested back.

"Okay, I got it. Let me go. Send me your update."

"Already did, Older One. Later."

The next hour passed me by. The admixture of vodka swigs and manic creativity stole time from my brain. As soon as I typed "Chapter Four," I heard the front door open. My antagonist had returned. Brown skin and sharp eyes that could snip a man's ego from below the waist under a salt-and-pepper 'fro. A mouth carefully painted with blood-red lipstick in a perpetual frown. It was a mouth that came with dimples, but it had been so long since she smiled at me I'd forgotten what they looked like.

"Nathaniellle . . ." The harsh screech of her voice rasped its way underneath my office door, grating my nerves like nails on a chalkboard. "Take out the damn trash!"

HEATHER

During my commute every day, I came to admire the Texas-style rustic home dominating the corner a few blocks from my house. I imagined the wooden beams hovering above the marble countertops in the kitchen. The all-black Harley-Davidson Iron 883 motorcycle immaculately cleaned, resting in one garage, while the other housed minivans and old furniture. The vintage living room where two children, a boy and a girl, would rest easy near a fireplace reading different books, both of equal creative stature.

In the upstairs master bedroom the wife would emerge from a mist of shower steam, ravishing, fresh, wrapped in a towel. She'd bend over and shake her hair wildly, then in a ferocious stance throw it back. The husband would loosen his tie, kick off his leather-soled shoes, and without taking time to fully remove his pants he'd sweep her into the bed, slamming her on her back.

She'd fight in a serious way then transform into casual submission, enraging his passion until his pants fell below his knees and he entered that paradise worth dying in. She would contemplate, her heart bursting beneath him, her eyes rolled back, having to sink her teeth into the towel she had just thrown off, now dangling on the edge of the bed. The mattress would rock with such intensity that the undisciplined husband would moan and cry out. The children would hear their parents intertwined in the supernova of—

A horn blared behind me in traffic. I'd been staring at the house so long I had missed the entire duration of a green light.

"Hey! Move out the goddamn way!" someone yelled from the rolled-down window of his car.

"Sorry," I whispered, before running the red light.

Daydreaming was my worst bad habit, next to my imaginary friend, whom I named Rose when I was six years old, who had stopped speaking to me last week. If I close my eyes I can still see her, sitting ethereally in her wicker chair in the basement, telling me the future with words that manifested from wisps of smoke escaping from a Tibetan sound bowl she played.

Traffic was brutal, but I finally made it back to my boring modern home, which lacked all the personality and charm of my Texan Dream House. Something from an IKEA catalog that even impoverished people would look over. Every day I sat in my driveway for an extra ten minutes, contemplating my situation. Pondering what life on the road would be like. A pariah, a deadbeat mom, sailing the seven seas, telling tales of ennui. But instead of backing down the driveway and speeding off into the night, I called my husband and ran through all the essential tasks of the day.

"Took you that long to answer the phone? I could've been dead by now," I said dramatically, waiting for him to give me a reply that could lead to something greater.

After his standard words of blah, blah, blah, I revved the engine and observed myself in the rearview mirror. I saw the hollowness of my smile that used to win over a room. A face that swelled after thirty-five, the dead eyes of a woman strangled by routine, murdered by monotony. I whispered the Prayer to The Orishas as I carefully backed out of my driveway, and went to Speakeasy, the nearby bar where a middle-aged woman could get a few winks and free shots.

To say it was a bad decision would be an understatement. Every man in the bar reeked of weirdness and desperation. I could see stink lines of perversion emanating from their skin. But I'd wasted twenty minutes getting here, so I felt I deserved a drink.

"Never seen someone like you in here before," the bartender said.

He had a dead eye but wore glasses. An immense gut poured over his belt.

"A Mojito, please," I replied daintily.

"Anything for you." His lips stretched upwards into a leer and I caught a glimpse of crooked yellow teeth.

When the mint leaves touched my lips and I tasted the rum, I reverted to what I always do: I thought about my child. After two more sips, I thought about my husband. After the third, I pushed the drink away, got back in the car, and drove home.

LUDWIG

Pain was what I was missing. I hadn't had any real-world experiences. I'd only kissed my first girl three months ago. And though she wore braces, was a little stumpier than I'd like, and may (or may not) have been a distant cousin, I still lied to my friends all the time about my male prowess. Even though I felt not one tingle in my balls.

"I just don't like her," I said to Ace in the cafeteria, munching on a sandwich. "I already had the hot girl. I need the smart girl now."

"Angel . . . Angel Hernandez. You're telling me, to my face, that you don't like or are in any way hard for Angel Hernandez," Ace shot back, sipping his apple juice like a man.

"She probably doesn't even like me." I looked down as I said it, concealing the fib.

"Dude, she's staring at you right now. Literally right now. If I were you I'd walk up to her, put my foot on the chair, pop a boner, show her the goods, then look her in the eye and say, 'You having my babies.'"

"Let's break down everything wrong in that sentence," I said in an attempt to change the subject. "First, it's harassment. Secondly—"

"Dude . . . dude." Ace held up a hand that was covered in grease from his pizza. "It's only harassment if they don't like you. My parents met at work. He was and still is super creepy. If my mom didn't like him, he would've been sent to HR immediately. Women have that power over guys. And she clearly likes you."

"Point taken," I admitted reluctantly. "But still, what makes you think she likes me?"

"Because she's always staring at you."

Ace was right. For the life of me, with all the intellectual and emotional intelligence I had, I couldn't tell the difference between a dog licking my face and marriage. I needed experience, which only reinforced my desire to leave home and seek it out.

When I got home, I began mapping out the departure times for buses and trains. Figuring out the farthest distance I could go, where to some degree I could still feel safe. Once again, like an idiot, I attempted to converse with my father.

"Dad?"

"Yea," he grumbled, staring at the bikini models fighting terrorism in the *Babes versus Iran* TV show, which couldn't have had a dumber name.

"You ever feel like you haven't lived enough? You know what I mean? Where people tell stories about you?"

"You alive, ain't you? In this big-ass house. Eating all my goddamn food. I tell stories about you every day."

"I mean real stories. Where I can walk in a room and say, 'This one time in Brazil, I met a woman during Carnival who taught me Portuguese in the Anaconda wine bar at the Saratoga Hotel.'"

"That's in Cuba."

"You get my point."

My father struggled to get up from his chair. He only moved when he was serious about something. I thought I'd gained some traction.

"When I was fourteen, all I did was ride bikes, play ding- dong-ditch, and steal *Playboy* magazines from your grandfather's barber shop."

"What about comic books?" I asked. "And all those strange novels? I heard you stopped writing in college."

"Who told you about that?" His voice rose slightly in surprise.

"Mom."

"Yea, okay." His broad shoulders moved up and down in a slight shrug. "That's part of it. But you leave those things behind. You grow into a man, get a lifestyle that's more about providing for women, then . . . comic books . . . sci-fi novels . . . slip through the cracks. You see, the problem today is . . . I . . ." My father was struggling to find the words. "Simply put, you're too damn young."

"I'm going to be fifteen in no time, arguably the peak of my teenage career."

My father scowled. "Go play ding-dong-ditch," he said and slumped back into his chair, diverting his attention back to the TV.

I stood my ground and retorted, "You realize I'm mentally too advanced for such childish things?"

"Then go write a theory on time travel," my father muttered, waving a dismissive hand. "Whatever. I don't know. If it makes you feel better, I feel the same way you do now."

NATHANIEL

Once my son left, I was free again. It was always weird staring at a miniature version of myself. He had my face but his mother's scowl and was growing his Afro in a style similar to hers. There were dark circles under his eyes, too, but he hid them with glasses.

Low on vodka but high on ideas, I began to write.

With translucent skin and elongated limbs, the Eleon stretched its claws to gently feel the human skin of Captain Nova. He quivered in the cave. Wait, quivered? No, he trembled in the cave, realizing his blaster had no more energy left to defend himself from the massive swarm that surprised him. The Queen Eleon slithered into the scene and produced a ray of light from her finger. Like E.T.

Wait, no. I backspaced the end of the sentence.

The Queen Eleon opened her mouth and projected a beam of light on the cave walls, and that's when Captain Nova saw it. Early blueprints of pyramids, math, and to the best of his knowledge, the Pentagon.

My phone rang in my pocket. It was my brother. I answered.

"Older One, it's 1918 again. Philadelphia, Spanish flu."

"You're not buying into this, are you?" I asked. "I just got over the flu in January. And that was the first time I've had the flu in over fifteen years."

"It will be a glorious sweep over the human race. If my prediction is right, we will all be affected."

"COVID-19, I know," I said. "It's been buzzing. But you can't trust it. Information has become a religion. People search for what they believe in."

"This is not fake news," my brother said. "We will at least be able to work from home. But the others, I fear it's bigger than we anticipate."

"I think the Drudge Report is poisoning your brain," I retorted. "I was right in the middle of something."

"I think Twitter is destroying yours. I only come as an oracle. The end is near."

"You'd love that, wouldn't you?"

"I would be lying if I said I didn't get a kick out of watching the world squirm," my brother enthused. "America in particular. But I don't want anyone to die.

Especially not you, Older One. But just because I'm a nihilist doesn't mean I'm heartless."

"I'll look into it when I'm done," I said, placing my fingers on the keyboard again.

"Do me a favor."

"Stock up on booze?" I asked.

"That won't matter. What you need to do is stock up on masks and gloves, before they're all gone."

I hung up the phone without saying goodbye and narrowed my focus back on my story.

Captain Nova's mouth was wide open. *No, aghast. Yes, Captain Nova's mouth agape, as he . . . he . . .* Goddamnit. I saved the document, shut down the computer, and wandered back upstairs.

On my way to the porch, I walked past pictures capturing every achievement in my life. Birth, high school graduation, college graduation, marriage, my child, then my child's accomplishments. I lived a linear life. Nothing was up to chance. Somewhere in the murkiness of the years, I'd sunk into a hole deep enough to swallow me whole.

Now I spent my days lost in the words of a space narrative, attempting to finish the manuscript before the national competition closed in a few months. I'd become so good at hiding my ambition that my wife believed I was searching for fishing poles to buy and porn sites to scan. It was better that way. Better if I stayed in the shadows. My son wanted to live in the sun, like his mother. At times, I tried to tell him that the light was a scary place to exist because the whole world sees your every move. I tried to explain the scrutiny I felt at all turns. The judgment, the resentment, the bitterness, how no one takes me seriously.

It was my own fault. I admitted it to myself just a few days ago because I present only a caricature of myself to the world. It's all they'll ever know about me. Somewhere in the journey, I split into three people. The father my son laughs at. The husband my wife gawks at, and the real me that's getting harder and harder to find.

I used a lighter to pop open the cap on my cider bottle. Beneath the chair I sat in, hidden inside a book,

I unearthed my five-year-old pack of cigarettes. About ten left. I only smoked them when things felt heavy. I sparked one, took a long pull, and resisted the knee-jerk reaction to look at my phone. I just sat in the silence and enjoyed it. Whatever was going on with the world didn't matter to me. I blocked it all out, drank more cider, and let the ideas flow into my head. *Enigma Space Corp.* was going to be my masterpiece

HEATHER

I stared at my client's face for so long in the video conference that her words began to sound like a refrigerator hum. It was my twenty-fifth hour, too much overtime, but money has a way of making you forget. I felt my eyelids getting heavy. I had that bubbling urge to close them and float back to that rustic house on the corner. Revisit my fantasies about my parents' passion behind their locked bedroom door. I shook my head, forcing myself awake.

"Be right back," I said, turning my video off and muting my audio.

I mumbled a prayer I'd created for myself for times like this. The bright fluorescent lights of the kitchen helped. I perused my choices in Keurig coffee pods: Starbucks caramel, Folgers classic roast, Green Mountain dark magic. I liked the magic part of this one's name.

While my coffee brewed, I watched an apparition form next to me. The specter resembled a regal, shapely woman, draped in jewels, floating in a luminous dress. It was Rose, and at the sight of her my heartbeat calmed itself back down. Never did I question the relationship I had with my imaginary friend. It was the by-product of loneliness, and even at my age I still felt lonely.

"*Agis ut cavaert*," Rose said, before moving out the window to soar over the city lights and the poor souls stuck in the capitalist system.

"Nice to hear you talk again," I responded in my mind.

I sat down again at my desk, put my earbuds back in my ears, and unmuted the audio.

"I'm back," I said.

"Heather, yes, just to catch you up," my client said. "We're working on disaster recovery options and possible work-from-home policies for the upcoming week. Or, if it continues, the next months. Do you have hardware in place? Laptops, tablets, maybe even take a look at the VPN setup? Have the users remote from their home desktop into the office?"

"Yes." I nearly choked on my coffee and my lie. There was no new hardware. Not wholly a lie, but still.

"I'll have my team work on it, but may I ask what all the caution is in regard to?"

"You haven't heard of the coronavirus?"

"From 1965?"

"Uh, I think it's the same one. Due to recent reports from China, it's spreading worldwide."

"Influenza is influenza. It'll be gone in a week."

In the parking lot, I saw Rose again. She placed a hand over her face and dissolved. The early prickles of a bad omen were settling into my bones. But by then, I was back in my economy car, enjoying the absence of late-night traffic. That glorious stretch of empty highway, when you know everyone else is already home, and a good portion is about to be on their way out. I drove past Speakeasy, never stopped at home, but circled back to a new place instead. A lounge called Akene.

My coworker Janet had raved about it at lunch, licking her lips more than usual. She kept looking me up and down so much that I checked my face with my phone's camera, searching for a booger.

"You *have* to go," Janet confessed in an empty conference room, an open carton of Chinese food in front of her.

"Why is it called Akene?"

"I don't know," she said slyly. "Good margaritas, maybe that's why. They have a great drink there called Passionberry."

I stared up at the clock, watching noon tick away. "I can't keep drinking like this every night. I don't want to become one of those people," I replied.

"A drink by yourself twice a week doesn't make you an alcoholic. It's regular. Shit, I go three times a week. But *never* go to Speakeasy. Not with Dead-Eye Willy. He's got another dead eye below."

"Janet . . ."

"I heard from someone else." Janet licked her lips. "Hold your judgment. Anyway, what's the big deal? It's Friday."

"It feels like escapism," I said.

"We all need it. And I'm alone. At least you have company when you go home. It's just Sparky and me."

"You have a dog too?" I asked. "What type?"

She laughed through a mouthful of food. "My vibrator," she chuckled, patting her mouth.

"I'm a digital girl, personally. Though I would prefer the real thing," I said, and felt the heaviness settle on my heart.

"Common." Janet patted my hand sympathetically. "More than you think. Ebb and flow with all things in life. I believe, as your friend, you need something new."

"New like what?"

Upon my arrival at the lounge, I was enamored by the bright purple lights swirling over the sign: *Akene*. I told myself to spend no more than twenty dollars, to wait no longer than thirty minutes. As I exited the car, I saw a missed call from Ludwig. He'd been distant lately, so the attempt at communication couldn't be ignored. I made a promise to give him attention when I got back. Maybe he'd like me more when I was tipsy.

There was a roar of '80s electropop encompassing the entire place. All around me were various shapes and shades of women. With no men around, I felt comfortable. A statuesque woman dressed all in black helped me get a barstool. Which was polite, but the stare afterward made me recheck my face.

"You look like a Mojito girl," the bartender said, winking at me.

"Yes!" I smiled, delighted. "How did you know?"

"I know everything," the bartender responded, moving away to fill my order.

Between my third and fourth sip, the band started playing. Heavy bass shook my feet. The entire floor was rumbling with the music. The woman in black took my hand and led me to the dance floor. Even though I didn't know the song, I tried my best with my two left feet. The woman smiled, moved in closer, and kissed at me. *Naïveté, thy name is Heather.* I blew a kiss back in panic.

I saw her eyebrows go up, and she hugged my waist. I didn't feel threatened, but there was a vast ocean of misunderstanding between us. Something that I couldn't put into words, so I tried to communicate it with my eyes. Well versed in the lesbian language I am not, because right after she kissed me on the lips.

LUDWIG

The day had come. Saturday, by midnight, I would make my move. Stealthily, I studied every motion, sound, and mood within the house. My backpack was full of clothes, two pairs of shoes, and a modest amount of underwear. Laundry didn't play much of a part in my plan.

By early afternoon, I had put phase one in place. The alibi. I would be at Ace's house till Monday. Since we attended the same school, his mother would drop both of us off. Ample time to travel, destination Rivertown. It was the most perfect mixture of rural and safe I could think of. Depending on my luck, I might even skip through a few states.

I spun around in my Workinglab Beta 5000 a few times. I tried to play a video game but my mind was preoccupied. I had missed messages from Angel on my screen. There was only one person I needed to communicate with. I dialed his number slowly.

"Yoo, you still coming over? I got Mountain Dew, pizza, and even a ten-year-old joint from my older cousin. Only half-smoked," Ace said jovially.

"The day has come, my friend. Have you forgotten?"

"Oh my god. Are you really doing this?" Ace asked incredulously. "Your parents are going to strangle you when you come back. I mean, if you come back. If I was a betting man, which I am, I'd say sex trafficking. You're going to end up in a basement in Mexico. Ludwig: the young and gorgeous power bottom."

"You watch too much news. But look, everything is in place. It's only an experiment. If things go south, I'll simply return, accept my punishment, and have 'the talk.'"

"You're a complicated fellow, Ludwig. If I were you, I would just walk up to my parents and say, 'Hey, I feel like blah blah blah. Because when I was six, blah blah.'"

"You don't understand my parents," I said. "Talking isn't really our thing. We speak with action only. I've seen my parents have a non-conversation over a big issue for fucking three weeks. I spent all those dinners listening to my fork hit my plate." I cleared my throat. "This will show them I'm serious. That I'm rebelling."

"Getting on the server later?" Ace asked.

"Were you listening at all?"

"Yea, yea, forks and shit. So you're at my house for three days?"

"Right," I said, "and I know our moms won't talk to confirm. Ever since that weird conversation last Christmas."

"My mom thinks your mom hit on her." Ace laughed.

"Ironically, my mom said the same about yours. Which is perfect. They'll never want to speak to or see each other again. So, we good?"

"You're going to leave without streaming today?" he said sadly.

"I'm only going to be gone for a few days. It will be my first story. The time I ran away from home—"

"And got kidnapped by Kangaroo Joe. He was so well endowed," Ace cut me off.

"All right, I'm hanging up. I trust you, Ace. Don't fuck it up."

"Fuck you. Anyway, watch out for the Wuhan virus. My parents can't even go back to the office next week. They keep teasing me about school being closed."

"Eh, the flu is the flu. Like swine flu, Legionnaire, it's fine." I paused, swallowed my spit. "Godspeed, old bean."

"May the pedophile be with you, old chum."

I hung up the phone and unfolded my large map of train routes. I had drawn arrows and lines to secure the fastest way to arrive. The J line at 8:00 p.m., transfer at Barrington Square, hop on the Transit line till the last stop. Then two buses and more subways. I should arrive by early morning and let the quest find me.

Two hours left before departure. I leaned into my computer, opened Notepad, and began writing a letter to my parents:

Dear egg and sperm donor, it is with a regretful heart that I say my life feels dull and safe. I want what you had.

I crave excitement. Being smart has only brought more emptiness.

After deleting the draft, I opened Angel's missed message: *Hi.* That's all it said, with three blue heart emojis. My hand twitched a little. I wrote a reply: *Next time you see me, I'll be cooler.* I deleted that draft also, removed "Find my iPhone" from my phone. Then I prepared myself for life without the internet, knowing that it could lead to me being caught.

In the center of my gray, shaggy carpet I sat and crossed my legs. Aside from the hum of my water-cooled motherboard I closed my eyes, basked in the somewhat silence, and entered my perfect state. During the mindfulness meditation I ruminated over my entire life up to this point of no return. All memory is relatively false, but I recalled as many details as possible. Twenty minutes later, I opened my eyes, my vision cleared, and I ventured downstairs to fool my parents by purposely exhibiting my everyday habits.

To my surprise I heard laughter, a playfulness even. Believing something to be afoot, I craned my neck around the wall at the bottom of the stairs. No fights? No liquor? They were sharing a glass of water between themselves, pushing it back and forth across the kitchen table. I moved in closer to hear what witchcraft had brought about this reunion.

"I know that place. Guys at the job call it the 'buzz cut.'" My dad laughed. "Should've took me with you."

"I don't think men are allowed," my mom responded, cackling. "I honestly don't even think I'm allowed."

"Got an admirer, from the way you tell it." My father smirked. "I wish someone would buy me free drinks."

"Right, two passionberries and I left. It's so irresponsible, Nathaniel. Somehow, this is your fault—you know that."

"It's not my fault you hit the curb outside the house and popped the tire." My father took a sip of water. "Crazy part is, I didn't even hear it. I felt it."

"Simpatico."

"That's not what that means, but I'll take it. We needed this." He motioned his hand to symbolize togetherness.

"We did. Hey, Ludwig, you look ready." My mom had spotted me.

"Yea, I'm going to leave early. Ace's mom—"

"Forget his mom; I'll take you. Come on. I'm in a good mood." She swiped her car keys out of a basket on the countertop. "You can get there early, surprise him."

On the car ride, my stomach did somersaults. I was more frightened by my mother's jovial mood than the entire plan itself. There was a hidden horror behind the smiles of my parents. I couldn't shake off images of them crying when they realized what I had done. But I had to go. I needed a diversion. Think, Ludwig. Use that brain, IQ 135.

While she hummed to herself, listening to an oldie and tapping the steering wheel, I hurled my first lie.

"Oh dang, I forgot to bring soda and chips. Can't show up without soda and chips. Ya know. The lifeblood of an adolescent teenage boy. Am I right?" I nudged her in the side like I was an amateur comedian.

She swerved a little and corrected the steering. "There's a million corner stores," she said. "I think Bushwick is a few blocks down."

"No!"

"Sorry?" My mother looked at me in surprise.

"I mean, no . . . they don't have what I need. It's the big bag. They have it in the 7-Eleven at the train station. Equal distance to Bushwick, similar pricing, better parking. In fact, just wait outside, I'll run right in. Spend some of that lawn-mowing money."

"Ludwig." She glanced at me, still driving. "Take it from someone like me, who's bad at lying. If you're going to do it, don't make yourself sound stupid. Don't give too many details, like the architecture of the bar, or what five patrons were wearing, or how many songs they played."

"Isn't self-claiming you're a bad liar the first step to being a good one?" I asked.

"Never thought of it that way. Also, omitting details isn't a lie."

"How so?"

"Because it's not that you lied, it's that they didn't ask the right questions. So, what's the skinny?"

I tried a different tactic. "I wanted to meet this girl before I got to Ace's. She's there right now."

"A girl?"

"Mom!"

"Just saying." My mother shrugged apologetically. "I've never seen you really go after girls. Well, wait, you're fourteen and I think that parenting book mentioned something like this. Are you sweating more? Easily aroused? Do you know what a penis is?"

Somehow, I actually blushed. "Oh my god, Mom. I knew that ten years ago."

"Sorry, I meant an erection. A hard-on."

"Jesus, yes, I know what that is. Don't say that! You know how parents always say, 'I accidentally messed up my children'? Well, this is how. This is the textbook definition."

"Do you get frequent hard-ons? Back in the day, we called them boners. Me personally, I always liked 'pitch a tent.' Even on a visual level, that works so well."

"Mom, please." I put my hands over my ears so I couldn't hear any more.

"What, dog?" My mother gave me a friendly little shove. "We can talk like this now. You're growing up. I don't want to be a distant parent. I want to be a cool one. Do they still call weed dope?"

"Mom! You're going to miss the train station."

"Oh, sorry."

My mother skillfully pulled into the train station parking lot, right in front of the 7-Eleven. I had to take off my glasses to wipe off the ocean of sweat accumulating on the lenses.

"I'll be waiting right here, dog," she said as she unlocked the car doors. "Hmm, everybody's wearing masks and gloves in there. Well . . ." She squinted. "By everybody, I mean the Asian people. They've been doing that since SARS, you know."

NATHANIEL

Somehow, while sharing a glass of water, I saw that twenty-five-year-old, cooky, weird girl who I had married more than a decade ago. I had plenty more to say, but less is the golden rule. I could've told her that Akene used to be called Yesterdays. I could've said that I randomly ran into an old friend of mine there six years ago, an Italian lawyer drinking away the woes of her single life.

I could've gone deeper into the story. About how we ended up going to the same house party. How something impregnated the air and space between us, minimized it to a microscopic level. About how toward the end of the night, we gave in to whatever dormant passion laid between us, bubbling from decades of platonic friendship.

About how the heavy kissing and touching evolved into a five-time coitus spree two days later. And how she ended the affair while taking my secret to the grave, respecting my significant other. I'd like to teach my son these tricks when the time's right. The unwritten laws of manhood. The act of killing your emotions.

How unearthing my only memory of stepping outside the lines had forced me to find a drink. Something stronger than water. Quell it all down, old man. Bring it all down, watch some dumb TV, fall back into character.

I checked my watch before turning on the TV, wondering why it was taking her so long to drop off Ludwig. As soon as I powered up the big screen I was bombarded with breaking news stories. COVID-19 was the buzzword, apparently. In one ear and out the other, I flipped back to *Babes versus Iran* and reclined my body on the couch.

My phone vibrated. I saw "Younger One" on the screen. I ignored it. Wasn't in a talking mood. I couldn't determine what mood I was in until I took my first shot of vodka.

"You're going down, Mr. Armed Forces," the blonde protagonist was saying on the TV. She held up the flamethrower strapped to her chest, which obviously was shown because she was wearing a bikini.

"Death to the infidels!" the antagonist screamed back, jumping off the pier. A cloud of flames behind him, not burning one strand of hair on his head. Amazingly, even though he dove forward, he landed right-side-up in a speedboat purring but perfectly still on the water.

"We missed him, Sarah. He's getting away. What will America do?" Mister comic relief recited his designated lines back to her. She had to lift an orange bucket off her head to even see straight.

The protagonist pushed her cleavage out. "Same thing we always do. Same thing America does every day. We're going to win."

I swigged another shot. Usually, a scene like this would bring me idiotic joy. Except right now I had a burning sensation in my gut. A latent feeling. *I miss my wife*, I thought, *and she's only been gone for thirty minutes.*

The doors to my house flew open as if pushed by a gale-force wind. Ludwig, with Heather right behind him. I stuffed my shooter of vodka between the couch cushions. That was another unspoken rule. Don't drink in front of the boy. After nearly gagging on the three sticks of flavorless gum I stuffed in my mouth, I spoke.

"Aren't you supposed to be going to Ace's?" I asked him.

He sent me a telepathic message while drooping his neck, holding a big bag of chips and soda. The message said: *I was trying to do something, but I failed miserably.*

"Your son lied to me today," Heather said in an upbeat tone.

"He's becoming a man," I responded, smiling.

Ludwig dragged his feet upstairs. "You still leaving at eight?" I asked him.

"Yea," he mumbled as he ascended the stairs.

I heard the water turn on in the sink. A glass placed on the table. A pitcher of water, leaned, filling the cup halfway. Heather passed it to me.

"Can we go back to where we were?" she questioned.

"It was about you, and this new habit of yours, because you're sick of me."

"Shh, don't bring the mood down. Let's go back. Back to when you were a hundred and ninety pounds," she said.

"You mean ancient times? I'm already there." I took a drink of water and pushed it toward her.

She sipped it, keeping her eyes on me. "I couldn't stay away from you then. Now, I don't want to step inside my own house with you in it."

"Don't forget the boy."

"He's tolerable. He'll change like the weather. He's not"—she squinted her eyes at me—"an old dog."

"So, I'm old now?" I chuckled.

"I am too." She smiled at me over the glass. "When Ludwig leaves, let's pour some wine. Go upstairs. Light some candles, maybe?"

The bold invitation caught me by surprise and I reached for the glass, flustered. "Why you gotta bring it up, Heather? Just let it happen."

"I tried that for three months."

I hung my head at that comment because every word of it was accurate. I'd grown difficult over the years. I had remastered myself and never thought twice about who it could affect. Self-preservation taught from my daddy. Who, in his own right, was the most selfish person I'd ever known.

"Okay. Candles and wine. I'm bringing vodka," I replied. "Can I tell you something?"

"If it's about that stupid story, I already—"

"No, no." I held down my hurt at the fact that she thought of it as just some stupid story. "No, I had a false awakening last night."

"Sounds mystical." My wife leaned forward. "I'm all ears."

"So, basically. I have a dream where I'm at some house, trying to play a card game, but I half recognize the people there. For some reason, they're hitting on me. Winking, tugging me. Some woman whispered, 'You must drive your mom crazy, with that dong.' And I'm genuinely freaked out. I think I wake up, I see you lying in bed. I tug at your headscarf. Excited to tell you, but then a fox jumps through the window. I wake up again, back in bed, looking at that headscarf. This time, I pull it off and you argue with me. But I wake up again and I'm back in bed. Now I can't tell the difference. Suddenly I hear all kinds of noises, sirens, footsteps of many people, car horns, et cetera. I think I'm going crazy, having an auditory hallucination. I reach for you again, but my arm doesn't move. I wake up again. My whole left side is stuck—it won't respond. My heart races; I think I'm having a stroke. I can't even get to you this time. I wake up again, convinced that I'm paralyzed. I know I'm having a stroke, and when I closed my eyes I saw all pink with a pair of red lips in the middle. When it opens, I see black, with white lines running through it. Finally, I think to myself, *This is death, and death is strange.* I allow myself to die. "

Heather finished the glass of water without passing it. She poured another and began to drink. I continued. "At this point, I can't tell whether I'm in the real world. So I grab on your shoulder. I squeeze it, and your alarm goes off. You move, and I hold you down. Finally, when you squirm away, I know I'm awake again. My heart was pounding. It was the scariest moment of my life."

"Why did you wait to tell me until just now?" Heather asked. Her face was a mixture of fear, concern, and confusion.

"I thought no one would care."

HEATHER

It was raining when I peeked outside my window at Ace's mom picking up Ludwig. I could barely see the car, but I remembered she drove a minivan. There was so much wind on the road earlier. A storm on the horizon. Such a bizarre woman, Ace's mother. To each their own, I suppose. On late nights, I imagined her seducing her husband, scantily clad, leading him blindfolded into their masonry-wall basement. Inside, chains draped from the ceiling, latex clothes with the crotch purposely cut out. A wall placement for an assortment of whips, sticks, and other phallic-shaped items. She'd flip a switch and a variety of red lights would gleam in the subterranean darkness. A seemingly ordinary housewife's secret sex dungeon in the basement. It was something in her eyes. Rose agreed—the woman was deviant. My secrets could never compare to hers.

At the edges of the bed on our designated sides, Nathaniel and I sat, not looking at each other. Plus, we wasted five minutes peeing out the absurd amount of water we'd drunk together. I reached for his hand and felt the cold glass of his vodka bottle.

"Don't get it on the bed; it'll make it wet," I scolded him.

"Sorry, I was about to drink it."

I heard him swallow and set the bottle on the floor. "I'm going to say something weird," I started.

"Right, like ancient times."

"Yes, the rain made me think about this story my mother used to tell me at night."

"About not to marry the man with the big dong?" Nathaniel laughed. "We've all heard that story."

"I think it was called Matt Wong: The man with the big—"

Watching Nathaniel smile at my joke warmed my heart. I missed that. Partly my fault for slipping into the monotony of regular life. Following all the rules people set in place for me. All those failed attempts at being the good girl who turned into the good wife.

"I gave you the comedy, now here comes the weird." I turned toward him, bent over with my knees in the bed like an animal.

He responded with his own stupid pose, one leg up, his hand over his head like he was on a ship looking at a foreign land, waiting to conquer it.

"Mbaba Mwana Waresa," I said slowly.

"Putting a spell on me? Doesn't work on drunks. Shamans hate vodka. Vodka and black people."

"Shh." I waved at him to be quiet. "So, Mbaba Mwana Waresa was a fertility goddess in the Zulu religion. She lived in the clouds." I waved my hands to mimic the sky. "And had a small house made of rainbows. Anyway, when the worshippers below would hear her thunder drum, they knew much-needed water would rain from her home. That water fell in our glass today, and we shared it."

"I see." Nathaniel seemed unsure how to respond. "It was much needed. I'll admit that." He swigged from the bottle again. "I'd be lying if I said . . . anything else."

"The story goes that she couldn't find a husband in the heavens. So, she came to earth to look for one." I stared him in the eyes and crawled closer to his face. "And she found him."

"How'd she find him? A big rain flood? His boat crashed into her rainbow hut?"

"Doesn't matter. What matters is how she tested him. She sent a beautiful woman to the man she loved, and

Mbaba changed her appearance to an ugly hag. Without hesitation her man was able to recognize her and they lived happily ever after." I gently grabbed Nathaniel's face. "Do you recognize me?"

"To be fair, Heather, you're far from an ugly hag."

"I watch you. I see those women on TV. I see their CGI bodies."

"Plastic surgery, dear."

"Do you see me?" I took off my shirt and bra. "Do you remember me?" I slipped out of my pants.

A small fire flickered in his eyes. He looked down before making eye contact.

"Yes."

"Then let's go back to ancient times."

LUDWIG

I counted about fifteen Louis Vuitton insignias on a random person's expensive face mask at the train station. I ended up spending an extra ten dollars on an Uber XL, the bigger one, and instructed it had to be the same model as Ace's mother's car. Phase one was complete. I was out of the house. Alibi intact. Gazing up at the giant schedule of the trains made me nauseous. All that planning and everything was delayed. There was an almost zombie-like atmosphere in the building. Everyone was spaced out more than usual. A few stares from strangers. A decent number of people were wearing masks.

I traversed the labyrinth, searching for the right track, afraid to ask an adult. Don't ask me why, but I assumed they all knew each other, and every last one of them was a snitch. Eventually I found myself in Sector B, with a platform between tracks ten and eleven. Above me I marveled at the perfect architecture. Tempted to use my phone, I killed the urge and put it in airplane mode. Staring upward I counted every beam, noted the curvature, observed every small shop with its overpriced goods, the faded, pink expired tickets littering the floor.

An intrusive thought sent a whisper of regret down my spine. *I wonder if my dad notices things like I do?* I shook it off, made my way to the ticketing machine. It was a multicolored puzzle, *Tetris*-like. I held up the line searching for where to put my crumpled five-dollar bill.

"It won't take it," I said to an angry mob behind me. "Keeps pushing it out."

"You gotta smooth it out," one patron said.

"Move out the way, I'ma be late for work!" another yelled.

"This motherfucker is going to make us late. Move!" a third, and clearly the most irate, screamed.

I panicked and dropped the bill. As I bent to pick it up, a wave of "Oh come on," and "What the fuck?" invaded my eardrums. Defeated, I stepped out of line.

"Thank you!" the irate one said, using the kiosk with a proficiency I found fascinating. Either he ironed his bills or he had the steady hands of a surgeon. Five minutes later, the line was clear again. I spent the time rubbing the five dollars across my knee, straightening it.

"Okay, Ludwig, IQ 135, okay, okay. You can do this," I uttered aloud, my mind running as fast as the train I waited for. "Okay, okay, one more . . ." The five tore right at the top-center, nearly splitting Lincoln's face in half. "Bollocks!" I yelled out loud, as my train roared into the station. "Shit, shit." I rummaged in my pockets, took out another five-dollar bill, and started all over.

"Don't rip that one too," a familiar, sweet voice said behind me. "If you ask me nicely, I'll do it for you, and I won't run off with it. I mean, I'm going to miss laughing at you. It's kinda funny, watching you struggle. For such a smart asshole you're bad with your hands, huh? In my imagination, you were better than this."

Without turning or thinking, I said, "I'll have you know I'm near-virtuoso on both piano and violin. I can even decant a bottle of Chateau Lafite Rothschild Bordeaux Blend to perfection. Obviously I've never sipped it, but from what I'm told—"

"Slow down, Antonio Galloni." The voice chuckled. "I didn't get to renew my subscription to *The Wine Advocate*."

"What?" I responded, irritated, finally turning around. When our eyes met, the five-dollar bill fell from my hand and fluttered toward the floor. Spellbound, I felt naked, stripped of the intellectual shield I'd spent years perfecting. She reached out to grab it and stuffed it in her pocket.

"Here." She motioned her hands, and instinctively, I handed her the ripped bill. She reached in her bookbag, took out a small roll of tape, repaired it, and put it inside the money slot. "Where are you going, Bigwig?"

Glimpses of my mother flashed before me, combined with a rapid heartbeat, and I heard wedding bells in my head. Logically I was lost: no conclusions, no theories, no nothing. "Angel?"

Angel raised an eyebrow. "He knows my name."

"What are you doing here?"

"What are you doing here?" she mimicked.

I folded my arms across my chest. "I asked you first."

Angel smirked. "See how that goes?"

"What? No, you're obligated to answer me first. It's fair and proper."

"In your big-headedness." Angel rolled her eyes. "In my mind, I just shrank you down to a small puppy I'm going to smuggle into my bookbag. I plan to feed you organic food, give you two walks a day, constant belly rubs and maybe a game of fetch if you're lucky."

"What?" I protested. "No, this makes no sense. For starters, therianthropy doesn't exist. Furthermore, the most common would be either Skinwalkers or, if I suffered from lycanthropy, which would mean I'd turn into a werewolf, so hypothetically, I'd be able to rip out of your bookbag with ease and escape to the woods. If any of this was possible."

Angel shook her head. "Hmmm, no, you'd be my puppy, aptly named Bark Twain or Prince of Barkness. Sorry to break it to you. My uncle turns into a dog every night. Doesn't seem to be hard."

"I see you're joking. This is all a long, clever joke. Well, remind me to laugh when I find it funny."

"I have magical powers too." Angel smiled.

"Please, digress."

"Observe." Angel snapped her fingers, and my five-dollar bill ejected itself. "Do you doubt my prowess now, Bigwig?"

I grabbed the bill and tried reinserting it. The machine pushed it back out. I squinted at her; tried three more times, to no avail.

"Say sorry," she whispered, grinning like the Cheshire cat.

"It is a machine," I pointed out. "Magic doesn't work on machines." I tried five more times when suddenly a new mob began to form, waiting to pay their fare.

"I could let the people eat you again." She took out a bag of popcorn. "Or submit."

"This is nonsense!" I pushed the bill too far in, and not only did it eat it, but it didn't register. The 0.00

balance stared at me, mocking. With a sliver of green showing, I gripped the bill with my fingertips. I took one steady pull; it ripped. The five dollars was gone forever.

"Stupid kid broke it," a stranger said.

"Someone find a worker here. Fucking asshole broke the thing," said another angry traingoer.

I heard them shift to the other machines. As I stood in defeat I looked Angel in the eyes, took a deep breath, settled my heart, and opened my mouth.

"Okay."

"Okay, what?"

"Okay, I'm sorry."

"Good dog." She snapped her fingers again, and the entire mangled bill was ejected from the money slot.

NATHANIEL

The vodka had its way with me, per usual. My favorite white girl. Stealthily I slipped out of bed, leaving a satisfied Heather snoring loudly. In the bathroom I popped two aspirin pills. Carefully, I lifted the top of the toilet tank, keeping my ear close so as not to make the clinking noise. Bobbing in the water were two small plastic bottles. Green tea and apple cider vinegar. Hangover cure of champions. I guzzled them down and made my way to the study downstairs.

My stomach settled itself as the computer hum kicked in. Like a symphony, the fans spinning, all the small beeps after, then the random operating system noises. The startup programs. The *StarCraft* wallpaper. The antiquated trail on my cursor. Home, thy name is Windows.

I opened my manuscript, scrolled through the first couple pages, landed on a problem area and reread, then edited until I caught up to the dreaded blank page. After cracking my knuckles, I simply wrote the word "The." I stared at it, forcing the hamsters in my brain to run the wheel and create a narrative. Two minutes later, I added "man" and took a break.

Back on the porch, the rain finally settled. Examining the eerie glistening from the still-wet paved roads, I sparked a cigarette. My phone rang; this time I answered it.

"Writer's block?" Younger One asked.

"Same time as always."

"Post-coitus, or pre-coitus? Whether alone or not?"

"I told you," I said, breathing out a puff of smoke. "Coitus alone isn't called that."

"It is for me."

"Post."

"Quite. Where did we leave off?"

"Captain Nova in the cave," I reminded him.

"We had decided on paintings on the cave wall, had we not?"

"No, we did." I inhaled. "I just can't seem to write it. The flow feels forced."

"You ever noticed that you have a habit of saying 'No' when you are actually agreeing?" Younger One remarked. "It's backward. Regardless, why not try a random scenario to get your fingers moving, then simply erase it. Have the cave . . . uh, cave in?"

"Already had that idea."

"Okay, what have you been feeling in the last eight hours?"

I thought of my recent talk with my wife and exhaled another puff of smoke. "A lot of things."

"Imbue it into the character, then combine it with the plot," Younger One suggested.

"Getting along with my wife for the first time in a month doesn't exactly fit into a space-fleet captain discovering a cave on a distant planet," I pointed out.

"Doesn't it?"

"Wait." A spark of creativity hit my brain. I stamped out one cigarette and lit another. "I think you're on to something."

"Try explaining that the paintings show a side of alien life we never see."

"Such as?" I asked.

"Alien romance, family. Surely they have some connection with the advancement of their species," Younger One said. "Yet, all we ever see is war and destruction."

"I'm not writing a romance," I said firmly.

"Poor, poor Older One." Though I couldn't see it, I could imagine my brother shaking his head in disappointment. "All great stories, preferably, the ones that matter, have a level of romance. The love of a boy and his dog. A captain and his ship. An assassin and his guns."

"You sound like my son. Always right, I'll give you that," I acknowledged, "but always delivering the answers in a snobbish way."

"A side effect of genius." My brother chuckled.

"Keep calling yourself that, see what happens."

There was a pause on the line. "You sound like Dad."

"I'm surprised you remember him. He died when I was seventeen. You were what? Six? At most."

"Ten. I have a better memory than most. The strange part is, even though he died at a critical stage in your development, somehow you turned out to be just like him without even having him around."

For once I had no smart-aleck retort. "Family is a funny thing."

HEATHER

I awoke in the middle of the night, physically alone, but spiritually an overwhelming presence was in the bedroom. Rose glowed iridescently in her wicker chair, watching me lie in bed. The frequency of her latest visits reminded me of my childhood. I was never sure if it was a relationship born of trauma or imagination. If the loneliness, the destruction of my nuclear family, or the scheduled time with a designated parent had forced me to overcompensate.

I remembered believing it was my fault. Somehow, I'd messed up, and this was my punishment. I remembered occupying the space my dad left vacant. The horror movies I shouldn't have watched at ten years old. The eerie gut feeling I always got when my mother tried to hide pain behind laughter. The dreams I tried to ignore that were really premonitions. Throughout it all, the only thing I found strange was how Rose and I both had aged. In my teen years, I speculated if she would ever die and send me back to that lonely place.

Except Rose never did, and she convinced me that I was enough.

Now, as a grown woman, I looked at her with childlike wonderment, awaiting her otherworldly wisdom. She puckered her lips and blew gently. Musical notes manifested out of thin air, dancing toward me.

"Is that a love song?" I asked, smiling.

"Mutata Revertetur."

"Who? The big one or the small one?" I watched, entranced as the notes circled my head like cartoon birds, still dancing.

"Both," Rose answered.

"Better or worse?"

Rose simply nodded her head and disappeared. With her departure she sucked the air out of the room and I had to escape to breathe. Wrapped in my favorite robe, naked underneath, I wandered to the living room. Beneath his study door I saw a sliver of light, my husband's calling card to be left alone. I tiptoed to the door, placed my ear on it. I could hear him typing furiously on the other side.

Nathaniel the Dog rubbed his nose against my leg. I scooped him up, scratched behind his ears, and made him my travel companion. I ventured back upstairs and entered Ludwig's room. The stench of male adolescence infiltrated my nose. My only child was an anomaly. None of us knew where he came from, not even him. In every single scenario, he had consistently gone left when we always went right. I used to tell him, all the time, that we were raising each other.

Sitting on his bed, I took in all the details of his space and inspected every nook and cranny. Expecting to find a hidden stash of adult magazines, even a rolled joint somewhere. All my first search unearthed were books on Hinduism, a half-full binder of old homework, and a strangely drawn formula entitled "The Hot and Crazy Girl Matrix."

I studied it for a few minutes before deeming it irrelevant and moved to a more unconventional search. Places a boy would hide things, specifically knowing where their mother would not look. I opened an old video game case and discovered the satanic bible. Not stunned at all, since I dabbled in the occult, I kept on. Walking over the rug a few times, I felt a lump near his computer desk. It was a plain notebook titled "Do not read." I immediately opened it.

LUDWIG

Every nail on her hands was a different color. The middle fingers were a combination of two colors. Sitting so close to Angel on the train, I kept inhaling harder and harder. It wasn't perfume. Maybe she was communicating to me through odors. I deduced it to be pheromones.

"Any allergies?" she asked.

"No."

"Good, because if you sneeze on this train, they're going to throw us off."

I looked at her and was momentarily distracted by the sweep of her hair. "Why would they do that?"

Angel blinked. "You don't use Twitter?"

"Discord and Reddit, mostly." I shrugged.

Angel looked around, then leaned closer and whispered. "Virus is going around. Everyone's beginning to panic. My parents started hearing about a quarantine on the horizon."

It was hard to focus with her face so close to mine. "In America? Highly doubtful."

Angel shook her head. "I got a really bad flu, like last month. Might've been that, but no one knew. You can't get it twice, right?"

"I don't even know what it is."

"Remember that answer," Angel instructed me. "Tattoo it in your brain. You'll be using it a lot. Especially with girls."

"I know girls." I looked away. "I know they're crazy."

"True. And I know boys."

I turned back to look at her face. "Oh, yea? Enlighten me."

"Ace called me when I was sick. It was the sweetest thing ever. He made this grand gesture about bringing me medicine and food and ice cream. Anything I wanted. Made me like him. Made him a little hotter in my eyes. And in that fantasy of a man doing whatever I wanted, I even got a little wet."

My face, though brown-skinned, took on a heavy blush. I shuffled in my seat.

"Thinking about it, aren't you?" she continued. "Me saying a dirty word." She leaned toward my ear. "What if I told you I was wet right now because I was thinking about Ace?"

I cleared my throat a few times. Spectators lifted from their seats, masks on their faces, and headed to another train car. "I can give you several reasons why I'm better than Ace. For one, he reads at an eighth-grade level. Two, he still has a security blanket. Three . . . I mean, Ace? Seriously. Do you not see this genius before you? I could do everything better than him. I could send you goods via a drone if I wanted to. I mean, if I liked you, of course."

"But, you don't," Angel pointed out.

"Well, on a platonic level, sure." As I said it, her pheromones grew stronger. "You did help me, and I intend to repay you twofold. Even if you are a witch."

Angel smiled and moved away from me. "See what I did there?"

"Of course," I said, although I wasn't entirely sure. "You shared an intimate secret with me, because socially, I am adept."

Angel shook her head. "I lied."

"Well, obviously." I paused, confused. "Wait, about what?"

"Ace doesn't have my number."

I stared at her. "I don't understand."

Angel's smile widened and she winked. "All you need to know is that I know boys."

"Nine stops until Rivertown," blared from the overhead speakers.

Angel checked her Apple Watch. "Damn. How many stops does this train have?"

"Twelve, but they get really spaced out after eight," I responded.

"Wake me at Rivertown." She put her legs beneath her, took off her hoody and made it a makeshift pillow.

"How do you know I'm going there?" I said, slightly offended.

"Because Ace told me." She yawned.

"Ha ha ha ha HA ha ha," I sarcastically laughed.

"You're going wherever I'm going. Isn't that obvious?" Angel barely got out the words, succumbing to sleepiness. "You're my puppy. Now guard me, Prince of Barkness."

"I'm sure this works on the rest of your concubines. But I'm not a pet."

Angel nudged me with her foot. "Shh, stop waking me up."

I opened my mouth to continue on, but her fake snore made me stop. Five minutes later the fake snores subsided into real snores, accompanied by snorts and a little drool.

With Angel actually asleep, I took out my phone. Still in airplane mode. Burning inside was the urge to tell Ace everything. Except, now, unbeknownst to him, our relationship had changed. I had thrown him under the bus. The second jealousy had taken hold of me. Which was illogical, petty, and childish. Yet, inevitable.

I took out the map and charted the course I was on. Circled at various points were parks I planned to sleep in. Sleeping bag packed; no tent though. Which was fine. There are no bugs in March, but there may be bums. Which was fine. Everything was fine. I could craft a weapon from a random piece of wood to protect me if conflict arrived. Plus, with more than enough rations, starvation would not be a problem. I was going to return home soon enough. This wasn't permanent, just an adventure. A test of myself to see something through.

"This stop, Middleburg," the conductor said over the speakers.

An inebriated couple stumbled inside and sat across from me. From the man's early male pattern baldness and the woman's hairstyle, I deduced them to be between their late twenties and early thirties. A foul stench of a cocktail made of several liquors emanated from the man's skin as he turned to look at me.

"That your girl?" he asked.

"An acquaintance of sorts, she is to me."

"Why do you always feel the need to talk, Shaya? Can't go three seconds without saying something to someone?" his girlfriend intervened. "Don't answer his questions, kid. It'll only egg him on."

I corrected my posture. "I accept the challenge. Ask away." I packed away my map.

"I like this little guy. Look at his face, Alo. All clear-eyed and shit. Mature. I respect that," Shaya said to his girlfriend. "You sleeping with her?"

"That's disgusting!" Alo said.

"Let him answer," Shaya interrupted.

"Of course not. She's my friend, not my sister. And she has her own home. Her own bed, too, I imagine."

"I only sleep with my friends." Shaya sounded proud. "True story, all the time. Sometimes in bunk beds."

"Are you homeless?" I asked seriously. "Because if you are, and you're going to Rivertown, I may need some information from you."

"Oh yea, like what? I'm from there. Born and bred."

"Well, what are the safest parks to sleep in?" I asked. "Or, perhaps, tunnels to sleep beneath? I'm weighing my options."

"Ohhh, options, huh." Shaya scratched his stubbly chin. "If I were you, right under 287. Cozy, barrels always on fire. Even a family of bindlestiffs. Cardboard boxes and markers galore."

"Fascinating," I said and made a mental note. "Rest assured, I wouldn't ask any other adult for this information, as I believe them to all be snitches. But from your character, I find you to be a poverty-stricken rake."

Alo burst out into laughter. Whatever expression of joy the man had had dissolved from his face. "I really like this kid," she announced.

"He's my boyfriend," Angel said, still snuggled up in her seat, with her eyes closed. "Only I'm allowed to like him."

"Hmm, and here you are." Alo eyed me over her boyfriend's shoulder. "Saying 'acquaintance.' Typical man, downplaying your emotions. Didn't mean to step on your toes, darling."

"Whatever," Angel grumbled, before going back to sleep.

"Hey, I know what poverty means. But what the fuck is a rake?" Shaya looked perplexed.

"Come on, let's leave the lovebirds alone." Alo motioned the man to get up, and they began walking toward the other train car. "Word of advice, kid. If she fights for you, she'll fight with you."

NATHANIEL

Ten pages. I'd composed ten more pages of glorious narrative. The vodka bottle was empty, but the creative high I was on sustained me. Several pops occurred when I stretched my back in the chair. A break would do me good. I wandered through the house in the darkness. My eyes lived here. They only adjusted when there was too much light.

The smell of the nocturnal air coming through an open window led me to the backyard door out of the kitchen. When I grabbed the knob, memories began to flow. Before things went sour in time. When I took one day off from fatherhood and Ludwig's train was already three stops ahead of me. I tried to catch up to him on a pedal bike, but we never arrived at the same destination at the same time.

After opening the door and stepping on the small concrete steps, I saw a vision of myself ten years ago when I had a garden: flower beds stuffed with roses. A more ambitious me, green thumb and all, deep into the soils with my hands.

To a degree I still dig, but only to bury. I'd gained a strange habit that not even my younger brother knew about. Over time, I gathered relics from my past—mementos, gifts, letters, jewelry—and I buried them in different places at different times.

I took the empty vodka bottle, placed it on the grass. As I dragged my feet to find the shovel, a creature galloped toward me, hoping for a midnight walk. I squatted to its level, stared into the animal's eyes, looking at the reflection of myself in them. Maybe we weren't so different after all. I glanced at the bedroom window, making sure the lights were still out. Perhaps Heather . . .

I knew what was next to go. Slipping into a stereotype didn't fit me. That adage of writers and drinking, losing the edge. Whatever madness in me that I transcribed through my fingers was there before and will remain. *This is only a sedative*, I told myself, *for months, years. It does not control me.* Before I sank the shovel blade into the lawn, a passing car illuminated something shiny near me with its headlights.

Hidden treasure. A silver medal for second place in a fiction contest. I was twelve years old. The first piece of myself I had buried. That dream was over. My healing came from a group of disgruntled winter chickens past their prime, congregating and conjuring fan fiction based on a discontinued show from the '90s. This is where I belong.

But who could've dug this artifact up? There was no indication of it in the grass. Everything was clean, not even a footprint. When I looked back, searching for the dog, I only found myself alone on the grass. Was the dog even here at all?

Beyond the medal, near the gate I had built, back when hobbies sprouted like the hair on my head, was a bottle with a letter inside. Against my own conditioning, I recognized it immediately. I shook it upside down, retrieved it, unrolled it. A letter I wrote to my father when the world controlled my vision. Full of blind hope. Details of what I'd do with the first book deal. How I'd spend the money on the family. Yada, yada, yada. I stuffed all of it under my arms; it was heavier than it should've been. Then I placed it in my study, nicely put together to be reburied tomorrow. With that in mind, I took myself back to bed. Heather shifted when she felt my presence.

"Where were you?" She yawned.

"On a journey to the past," I replied, slipping under the blanket.

"Funny you should say that. I took a trip as well."

"Oh yeah?" I turned toward her, held her like I used to ten years ago.

"I had a peek into the mind of our alien child," Heather said, her fingers twining around mine.

"Find anything worth mentioning?" I rested my chin on her head and caught a whiff of her shampoo.

"His mind is a labyrinth."

"So is yours."

Heather shook her head slightly. "Hmmm, more of a web for me. Woven by emotion, unfortunately. I told you my theory on that, haven't I?"

"I probably forgot, so you're probably going to tell me again." I rolled over.

"The difference between a man's mind and a woman's mind," Heather continued drowsily. "A man's mind is composed of several boxes, which grow larger in quantity as he lives. And he packs away every inch of himself into these boxes. When needed, he opens one box, but never all at once. Tries his best not to spill the contents. And he lives this way till death, compartmentalizing every fabric of his soul."

I wanted to grumble. Instead, a whimper emerged from my mouth. "Maybe."

"A woman's mind is a web of memory." Heather rolled over so I could feel her warm breath tickling my ear. "Always connected, never severed. We live all-time at all times. When something sparks a line of silk from fifteen years past, it will awaken an emotional response in the present. Everything is connected, and we are not afraid of it. We embrace it because all of it is us. We change, but we are who we are. The web is beautiful."

"And what of this alien child of ours?" I asked.

Heather sighed. "From what I can tell, he searches for parts of himself in a maze he's built but forgot the pathway to. By default, he lives every moment as an equation to be solved. And when he's confronted with a dark corner, he races the maze until he finds it. He doesn't live in the present. He lives in the seeking."

I turned back toward her. In the darkness, I could only make out the shadowy outline of her face. "I feel like that sometimes."

"If that's the case," Heather said, "Ludwig is looking for something ahead of himself, which is dangerous."

"We call that ambition," I said and heard Heather's sigh as she rolled away from me.

"I guess. What if he doesn't find what he's looking for?"

"Then," I said, hoping I was right, "he'll be an adult in no time."

HEATHER

I did to Ludwig what my mother did to me, and her mother to her, all the way back to the beginning of parenthood; when a caveman would carve intimate thoughts on a stone he believed would remain unturned. A periscope view into someone's psyche. Inside Ludwig's journal, every entry contained nothing but fears. Based on the dates, he'd started writing in it last year, which would match up with him going through puberty.

He saw me as a wounded warrior, moving robotically through the last years of cognitive life. It always tickled me how time was viewed by a child. Let a teenager meet a thirty-year-old; they'll assume that person's life is over. As if we all go through a spiritual grinder and come out on the other side a wholly formed adult. Unable to make mistakes, really just a distributor of rides, video games, inexplicably earned money, and snacks that keep appearing in the kitchen.

I made sure to put his journal back where I found it. For Nathaniel's sake, I prayed he'd never read it. Unflattering would be a compliment of what his son thinks of him. A Neanderthal energy vampire that orbits his carefully built solar system. A living cautionary tale. All of it was explained in the first paragraph.

Further in, it became clear how Ludwig didn't value himself. Somehow, his intelligence burrowed into dangerous thoughts that could not be unrooted. Two of them. The first was how his sole existence was the pursuit of my approval. Without consistently being on the honor roll and exhibiting a mild manner at all times, he feared I would disown him. He dove deeply into a particular night when he experienced, unbeknownst to himself, a breakdown. Where a "C" in Spanish placed him a panic. He spent the rest of the entry conjuring alternative means of living outside the house, exiled from the family.

Notes and theories on life in the outdoors. Quotes from Thoreau. Deep sadness about the fact that my love for him only existed because of what he could do for me, and vice versa. A warped symbiotic relationship that traversed beyond mother/son, into almost master/slave. Even the slashes of the lines where he wrote the words changed. Practically pouring out of him, a real cleansing of all that hurt.

I left two teardrops on that page in his journal. I was sure he'd find them if he ever read back through it. And if he did love me, he'd seek me to a private place, and say, "I am flawed." I would respond to him, "All the best people are."

Toward the middle of the journal, Ludwig discovered philosophy and wrote about liberation. He speculated about people who didn't live up to their full potential. The hazards of living a safe and secure life. He wasn't challenged. He worried that these were the ingredients of a spiritual grinder. Fearing he'd wake up a seventeen-year-old one day from death. An adult too soon, and a childhood forgotten.

I had to wrestle my hand with the other to not call or text. I needed to allow Ludwig emotional room to grow. He yearned for something I couldn't provide. He craved the freedom to make mistakes.

LUDWIG

"Last stop, Rivertown!" the overhead speakers blared.

I nudged Angel. Watching the drool flow down her arm was proof she was human, because at times it seemed doubtful. When I looked out of the train window, seeing nothing but darkness in all directions, no one on the platform, a small prick of solitude caught me off-guard. More than ever, I was grateful to have this witch-woman near me.

"Damn, why did you wake me?" she complained.

"This is it. We have to get off now." My voice broke.

"I had the most awesome dream," Angel grumbled. "You weren't in it. But shit, it was the best."

"So, where do we go now?"

"The genius abandons his master plan and goes astray?" Angel shook her head in disgust. "Bravo, Bigwig. This is the part where I, in the most clichéd of all ways, say goodbye."

Angel stretched her arms and back. My eyes wouldn't look away. She'd cursed me. Every thought

I had involved her now. Any idea held a disclaimer of "we" at the beginning.

"I have my maps. I have my rations. You would do well to team up with me. Plus, you're a girl," I said pompously.

"Right, right." Angel rolled her eyes. "I forgot about that."

"I have materials for a tent," I said. "And the quickest route to the safest park. The old guy gave me some good advice. We can go to 287. By morning, we can scour the town, take in the experience. Make a story out of it."

"Scour the town?" She laughed. "We're not on a honeymoon. I don't think you see what's going on here. And, forgive me if I'm wrong since I'm a girl and all, but I'm starting to get the feeling that you're a needy little bitch."

"How dare you!" I rose from the seat and almost fell forward when the train slowed to a halt.

"Come on, people, last stop," the train conductor said. "Time to go."

I hastily walked outside in a brazen attempt to get in front of her. I tightened the straps on my bookbag, located the stairs, and nearly jogged to get distance from her. Outside, the train station was an empty metropolis with cracked concrete in the streets, blinking streetlights. A few brightly lit bars with women's silhouettes on corners.

A stench of urine caused me to notice a line of homeless people sleeping at the station door. *Should've planned better*, I thought to myself, looking at their despondent situation. When I unfolded my map, searching for my next steps, I heard a familiar voice.

"Hey, little guy, where you headed with that old-ass map?" Shaya, from earlier on the train, asked. "You want to ride with us?"

"Oh my god, no," said Alo. "I don't want to be responsible for this kid."

"It' only right, babe." Shaya smiled, rows of yellow teeth. "He's lost. Look at him. He looks like a puppy."

I drew myself as tall as I could and spoke in the most dignified way manageable. "I am a teenager, not an animal. And I am not lost. I just need to prepare myself for the next phase of my journey."

"Next phase, huh?" Shaya smirked. "You wanna meet some interesting people along the way. Let's make a detour. House party about ten minutes away."

"Will there be food, and a sink, in which to brush my teeth?" I asked.

"Oh yea, we got plenty of sinks, food maybe." Shaya gestured for me to follow him. "Shit, I'll get you something fast on the way."

"I'm sure this is illegal," Alo commented. "But you don't want to be here by yourself. Not on this street. Hey, I get it, man. I was just like you."

"Just like me?" I asked.

"Yeah, dude, a runaway," Shaya answered for her. "Or, as you would call it, a truant. Don't forget your girl though. She's standing behind you. She can come too."

"My girl? You mean that incessant witch?" I said before turning around and seeing Angel's red eyes.

I don't know if she was crying or conjuring a spell, but immediately after, I saw stars in all directions. My knees struck the pavement. I slumped over to the side.

"Hell hath no fury . . ." Alo winced.

"Ugh," I managed to say, caressing my tenderized testicles.

"Take us to Hoover Street," Angel commanded. "If you'd be so kind."

"All right." Shaya eyed her warily. "But my stop first, then yours. I ain't no Uber. And if you try to knee me, I'm going to headbutt you."

"And I'll allow it," Alo added.

"I have money," I grumbled from the ground, seeing a homeless man in my blurry vision sleeping peacefully.

"Don't need money." He crouched down to me and pulled a wad of cash out of a tattered pocket. "God bless America."

I heard the pair exit. Despite being in no shape to walk, I prayed for their return. However, now alone with my assailant, a rage brewed. Angel circled me, vulture-like, watching me collect myself.

"You can leave now," I mumbled as the pain eased. Luckily she'd mostly hit my thigh. "Pretend like we never saw each other. Matter of fact, make yourself disappear. You're capable of that, I'm sure."

"I don't trust them," Angel said, ignoring me. "But a ride would do us some good. I forgot how slow the buses are this time of night."

"Either leave or apologize. Otherwise, I have no use for you." I pushed myself upright. "We're going to different places. I understand that now. No need to slow each other down."

"And leave you here to die?"

"Apologize or leave." I looked her in the eye. "I'm giving you an ultimatum."

Angel crossed her arms, her mouth set in a stubborn pout. "It's my knee that needs to apologize, not me; it's like it took on a life of its own." She bit her lip and looked away, seemingly interested in the passengers now milling around the station platform. "You left me," she said quietly, and swiped at something that looked suspiciously like a tear on her cheek.

Confusion strangled every word I tried to speak. I shook my head like a baby rattle to create new ones. Another spell afoot, I was sure of it.

"You told me you were leaving. Then you insulted me. And you're mad because I left you? What type of psychosis is this? You don't have the right to be mad! I'm the one that should be—"

"Hey, hey, hey, make love not fight," Shaya said, poking his head out the window of a half-painted Pontiac parked on the curb, a marijuana cigarette hanging out of his mouth. "Jump in the back."

"You like Ska?" Alo inquired, scrolling through her phone, preparing to play music. "Or Indie Pop? I feel like this is an Indie Pop moment. La maturite."

The man gestured at us impatiently. "Are you coming or not? I'm not hanging around here all night."

I jabbed a thumb in Angel's direction. "I hate this witch with every fiber of my being. Can I please sit in the passenger seat?"

All three of them laughed at me, almost like it was a practiced response. I purposely walked around to the other side of the car to get away from Angel. We opened the back doors simultaneously. Once inside, she attempted to lean on me. Her scent invaded my nose unpleasantly. I moved away, as close to the door as possible.

"This strange music you are playing. Can you please turn it up as loudly as possible, without damaging your stereo system?" I asked.

"Obvi," Alo said, as she turned up the volume.

I drowned in slow melodic acoustic guitar and esoteric lyrics sung as whispering vocals from two women. Out of the corner of my eye, I saw Angel blatantly gawking at me. I forced my line of sight out the window and took in all the details of Rivertown.

"What's this song about?" I yelled over the music.

"Suicide," Alo answered.

NATHANIEL

I awoke with the rising sun, as I always did when I drank, so every day for the past two months I was alert at roughly six in the morning. Every Saturday I'd sneak downstairs and catch the old cartoons for a solid hour. Nostalgia brought me comfort: knowing exactly the beginning, middle, and end of each episode. The older I got, the funnier they became. Not only did I sink into a happier time, but I caught nuances that were so blatant to an adult but lost on a child's mind.

I ate the same breakfast every day, one of those microwavable sausage-and-biscuit sandwiches, washed down with a screwdriver. Some days it all went down easier than others. Afterward, if no one bothered me, I'd grab a cigarette, play "So Long, Frank Lloyd Wright" by Simon & Garfunkel, then ritualistically add the flame when the flutes came into the song.

I'd forgotten I had left the window open in the kitchen. A mistake Heather would turn into a massacre. Except when I went to close it, there on the lawn in the backyard was every item I had buried, now on full display.

A "Do-It-Yourself" magic kit. Two pairs of filthy basketball sneakers. A binder full of sports cards. A telescope for children. A *Penthouse* magazine from 1990. Letters to Santa. The satanic bible. My early draft of a screenplay titled *Dying Single*. Before I could react, I saw the brim of my neighbor's hat bobbing above my fence.

"Doing a yard sale?" he asked. "I'll take that magic kit."

"No, just . . . just some old shit. I'll take care of it." I rushed outside, put another cigarette in my mouth.

"On the wagon again? I won't tell."

"Sure." I stepped into my past with the grass tickling my bare feet.

"Is that a real gun?"

"Cap gun."

"Where's the orange part?" my neighboor asked.

"I . . . I took it off."

"Hmm, surprised you even kept some of this," he observed, leaning on the fence. "I recognize that game piece. They stopped making those in the eighties. You some kind of hoarder?"

"Do I look like one?" I let the bluish-white smoke linger after I blew out the match.

"Do I?" He chuckled. "I do the same shit. Whole basement full."

"Bring me a black garbage bag, could you?" I asked, starting to pick up the mess.

"Okay, but for real, I'll buy that kit. In fact, I might even do the same. Sell my old soul at the end of the world."

I struggled to remember his name; we'd only been neighbors for ten years. Rocky? Clay? No. "Cliff. Hate to break it to you, again, for the millionth time." I walked close to him, spinning my cigarette in a circle. "See this? It's the earth, Cliff. And it's never going to slow down, burst into flames, or implode. There's no black hole coming from a dying sun to eat up the solar system. There's no lizard people. There's no aliens, chemical warfare, or nukes from China heading for your doorstep to kill you dead. Truth is, I'll give you this shit. All of it, for free. I don't want it. I fucking buried it."

"Well . . ." Cliff adjusted his hat. "That's kinda dumb. Obviously, the pyramids. I mean, writings are on the wall. Literally. And some of this stuff you can't sell. Is that an urn?"

As I dropped my cigarette, the cherry tumbled off my shirt, leaving ash. My body reacted on its own. Heart palpitations, constant blinking, a weakness in my knees. Right in the center a weathered brass urn, completely clean, with golden rings around the top and bottom.

"I didn't bury that!" I scrambled to pick up the cigarette and stub it out. "I thought I lost it."

At that moment I noticed the dog by the kitchen door casually walk back inside the house.

"Just bring me the bag, Cliff."

Cliff didn't move, eyeing the urn curiously. "Who's in it?"

"I think it's my father."

"You think?" Cliff gave me a look. "Deep. Well, I don't have any garbage bags. Knock on my door when you want to sell that kit."

His hat brim disappeared behind the fence, and I heard his footsteps go quiet. On a spiritual level, I felt obligated to kneel beside the urn, caress it. A burning need to open it. A culmination of the eerie things suddenly following me. I remembered every bad memory as my hand touched the urn's top. I revisited past events I spent time burying in my mind. The nights where I took my little brother outside with a change of clothes, explaining we couldn't go back home. Knocking on my grandfather's door furiously, in a panic. The smell of hot cocoa he'd made for us because it was mid-December. The infectious laugh he released when I finished a tirade about life being unfair.

"You're just like him," my grandfather would say. "He's trying to run from you too."

Hearing Heather's footsteps approaching brought me back to the present. I expected a barrage of complaints, intellectual insults, or subliminal jabs, some I wouldn't get until next week. Instead, she stepped through the items, bent down, picked up a Tea Forte cup, and gasped.

"Wow, I thought this thing was gone," she said as she put her finger through the handle. She sniffed at me and turned back toward the house. "Clean this up. And stop smoking."

The door slammed behind her. How did she not notice the urn? Maybe she had expected this? I truly questioned her mental state, but quickly snapped back to my situation. My hand shook as I opened the urn. Inside was a small gold key lying on top of the ash. Plucking it out and placing it safely in my pocket, I wondered what it went to. No treasure chest. Nothing that even needed a key. I heard Cliff come back to the fence.

"Know what? I changed my mind. I'll take that *Penthouse* too. Pages aren't . . . you know, sticky or nothing?"

HEATHER

Snug in my headscarf and black robe, I let my imagination drift into Nathaniel's newest story. I felt like Captain Nova, bloodied, staggering out of the crash. Checking my suit for a tear, marveling at the two moons above me. Smacking my leg to get the blood rushing back, limping toward the cave entrance. Dragging my heavy body through rocky terrain the color of burnt umber. I noticed my communicator hung busted on my wrist. Another failed mission. I'd be removed from the Corps when I returned. Not to mention the materials that were destroyed in the crash. Something shot me out of the atmosphere, purposely, calculated, waiting for me to enter the orbit.

All my equipment could do was emit plasma light to brighten my surroundings. There on the wall, paintings of alien origin. Multiple triangles, mandalas, hieroglyphs, equations that resembled rocket science. Suddenly, a cacophony of clicks, light footsteps, and a red beam illuminated the space around me. Beings appeared, tall and slender, with large bulbous heads that throbbed in sync with the clicks. I reached for my blaster, but the handle was broken in three places.

Nathaniel bumped into a table, dragging a huge black garbage bag filled to capacity. It jarred me back to reality. Unbeknownst to him, I read everything he writes. Every draft, every throwaway, typo; finished manuscripts, outlines, I was privy to it all. Time and alcohol had eliminated his stealth. His password, simple: a combination of his debit card pin, birthday, and some random special characters. My email was full of it all. Right under his nose. I didn't ask him any questions. I didn't need to. I was a secret admirer of his work.

I dipped my leftover French fries in a ramekin filled to the brim with ketchup. Soon as I turned on the TV, I saw a paused screen of his favorite wretched show: *Babes versus Iran.* A woman was firing two Uzis, her breasts right below her chin. Then, beneath my butt, a vibration. I sprang upward, clutching my phone, hoping to see Ludwig's name on the screen.

"Hey, girl. I was just calling to fill you in on the latest," Janet said on the other end of the cell phone. "Aside from me ending up stuck with a high-ass bill at the bar with my sister's friends. I'm like, why you drink all of that just to piss me off on the car ride home? I could kill us all, no problem. Over the hump and into the water." She stopped to breathe. "I should've said no. My gut was telling me no. But sometimes, I be trying to change. Everyone always be like, Janet, you need to change. And look what change got me, paying three hundred dollars at two in the morning. Shit, I dropped them both off at the wrong house."

"Classic Janet," I said, shaking my head in amusement.

"It was only a block away. They didn't even know it was the wrong house. I hope they okay. I haven't called them yet. Well, my sister didn't call me. So, you know, no news is good news."

"Stop hanging out with young people," I advised. "Too much gray matter in the brain. Can't see past their noses."

"You right. I be hoping you're wrong sometimes, so I can rub it in later. Voice of wisdom, my clearheaded Queen."

She heard me smile through the phone.

"What's up?" I asked.

"I don't think we're open on Monday. Looks like this coronavirus is spreading. Knowing John, he's going to open anyway. Except, I been hearing them yelling at IT about disaster recovery and work-from-home setups. If not this week, maybe early March or so, we're going to be stuck home."

"It's that serious?" I frowned. "Maybe I should get Ludwig. He's out at a friend's house."

"Not yet. I don't want to panic anyone. This information is coming from my international whistleblower."

"You still talk to—"

"No judgment," Janet interjected before I could finish. "Long distance has its perks."

"Probably," I responded, watching Nathaniel stick a key into a drawer in the kitchen. When it failed to turn the lock, he grunted and wiggled it back and forth until it finally opened.

"And phone sex."

I rolled my eyes. "Goodbye."

"You should try it," Janet suggested. "Call Nathaniel on lunch."

"Goodbye, " I repeated.

"Okay, call me later?"

I chuckled. "Obviously."

I hung up the phone, closed out the email with Nathaniel's story, slid my feet into my slippers, and started breakfast. I desperately wanted to talk about last night. About how deep the bond felt. Men are a strange breed. The surface level was easy to pick apart, but the subterranean level, now that was scary dark, and deeper than the ocean. Maybe we weren't too different, but Nathaniel wore his heart in his back pocket.

As the curtains fluttered, a cold chill kissed my neck. Goose bumps tattooed my arms. Rose ascended into the kitchen. She floated above the stove as I dropped some butter into a hot pan. She curled her finger to lead me to the Tibetan sound bowl. I ignored her at first, cracked the egg, added it with the butter, grabbed the spatula.

"In a second," I said to her.

"What?" Nathaniel turned at the sound of my voice.

"I was just talking to myself."

Nathaniel gave me a look that meant he didn't believe me. "Mmmhhmm."

When my plate of food was done I placed the ketchup bottle to my right, a glass of water to my left. Before I could sink my fork into the grits, Rose blew the cup of water off the table.

"Jesus Christ, okay!" I yelled, hopping up to get paper towels.

"Talking to yourself again?" Nathaniel asked again, a little concerned.

"Yes!" I scowled at Rose, who smiled from her place on Nathaniel's shoulder.

Nathaniel blinked in confusion. ". . . Okay."

On my knees, drying the floor, I heard the Tibetan sound bowl slide toward me. When I looked up, Rose pointed her finger down, signaling for me to put my face in it. We'd played this game before. I always hated it. The visions were puzzles every time. One of the first ones was simply a transcript of my junior year at college. Unable to understand it at the time, being eight years old, I'd misplaced the memory. Until the day I saw it on a computer in the library. Excited for the grades, eager to please my parents, begging to win approval, I accidentally yelped and stood up. When I did, Nathaniel, sitting across the desk, shushed me and smiled. It was the first time I'd ever seen his face.

Reluctantly, I placed my face inside the bowl. Watery at first, blurry images of an elephant tapestry draped on a wall. Incense burning in a living room. Everything smoky. On a coffee table a few spirituality books, one half-opened. A mash of flesh slowly forming into a human being sitting on a couch rolling a joint. Two more, bent over, straws in their hands. A white substance growing into a small mound before them. I heard Nathaniel enter the kitchen. He stopped and stared at me on the floor, face looking at the hardwood. Unable to see what I saw.

"What?" I growled at him.

"Nothing." He slowly backed away. "I'm going to Home Depot."

"What for?"

"I need to make a copy of this key." Nathaniel reached for the doorknob.

"What key?" I was already immersed again in the subjects taking shape in the bowl.

"Exactly," he said. I heard the door open and close as my husband left the house, leaving me to my visions.

LUDWIG

One hundred and twenty seconds. That's how long each streetlight took to change. We ran into about fifteen of them. Two, the driver irresponsibly ran, abusing the meaning of caution. I occupied my time by admiring the architecture of the downtown buildings. How reflections of light bounced off the rain puddles in the street.

At times the windshield wipers matched the music in the car, and deep inside I giggled like a child. Aside from the cigarette smoke, I grew to enjoy the older couple's demeanor. True, a kidnapping if authorities were to approach us. However, I'd immediately drop charges.

The gentle rumblings of any automobile still lull me to sleep. I rested once in a five-minute interval. Upon waking, there she was where I left her. Some strange version of the silent treatment, or reverse psychology. I kept steadfast. Angel never stopped staring.

"Jesus," Shaya said, looking for a parking spot.

"Shoulda went on the train," Alo replied in a sassy tone.

"Those restrooms are disgusting."

"Hear, hear!" I yelled from the back seat.

"You need to go too? Help me find something."

"They pile people in this area. Stacked up and up, yet everyone hates each other. Sweet inner city, how I've missed you," Alo whispered to herself.

"There's a spot ahead. Make a left on McKinney," Angel broke her silence. "I'm sure of it. Right behind an Acura."

"Left on McKinney," Shaya repeated, then followed the directions, saw the spot, parked immediately, and unlocked the doors.

"Turn the car off, Shaya," Alo snapped.

"Yea, yea," Shaya quickly murmured before stepping out. "Look around." He unzipped his fly as Angel stepped out of the car.

"Ew," Angel scoffed.

Shaya stopped, changed his posture, and reevaluated himself. "On about five different levels, this is wrong." He zipped it back up. "Alo, summon them. Please!"

When I emerged from the car, I saw Angel staring at a house on McKinney. From the side of her face, I noticed a clear change in her manner. Wasting no time in solving the Rubik's cube of her emotional state, I followed the couple to the corner.

My conscience tugged on my collar as the distance grew between them and me. I turned around. Angel was still staring at the house. A red light shone in the bedroom window, like a bloody eye, responding to her presence. Without looking at me, she spoke.

"This is my journey's end, Bigwig."

I eyed the room with its light like a crimson beacon. "That's how you knew about the parking spot."

Angel shrugged. "Or . . . obviously, I have magical powers."

"Or delusional."

Angel punched me lightly in the arm. "Did you know that hate and love are two sides of the same coin?"

"I prefer indifference."

Angel paused. "Remember when I spared you?"

"At the train station. Yes, and I expressed my gratitude."

"No, I meant my knee." She smiled wickedly. "I have all boy cousins. I know how to take down a guy."

I took a cautious step away from her, just in case. "Your words closed the gap. Wound intact."

She scratched her ear. A nervous twitch. "The back door is always unlocked."

"Is that a sexual innuendo?"

Angel shrugged again. "I'll be here unless you really want to sleep beneath the 287. With your tent and apple sauce rations. I'm sure your big male brain is going to be comfortable sleeping on the concrete." She sighed, running a hand through her hair. "Silly me, actually going to a place with a bed and pillows. But I won't hold you. Though, you should know, if that couple goes to the house where the doorbell is inside the painting of an Egyptian—"

"You're supposed to be letting me go," I interrupted her, "which I would appreciate."

Out of the corner of my eye, I saw Shaya peeing on a bush in front of another house as Alo kept watch.

Angel chuckled, shook her head. "I've met my cliché quota for today." She took her first few steps toward the entrance. "If you're not dead by morning, let me know how the kidnapping went. Spare no details."

"You'll be the last to know," I called after her.

The first thing I noticed was that Egyptian eye with the bell button for a pupil. As Alo rang it I heard no sounds; the door creaked open on its own. Shaya looked back at me.

"They're in a good mood. Better to have one visitor than two." She'd read my face. "You'll return to each other. Like magnets. I do not doubt that."

The hallway was long, with painted doors on both sides. Each had its own artistic picture. They also ran in pairs: men on one side, women on the other. To my right I saw an image of a very young girl in a flowing dress, standing in a field of daffodils, reaching for the sun. Based on height, I deduced her to be between five and nine. To my left, a little boy going down a slide, except instead of sand at the bottom, it was a whirlpool.

Part of me wanted to hold someone's hand. New is scary, but my story was being written right before my eyes. Instinctively Alo reached back, took my hand, and led me. Toward the end, the pictures grew esoteric and gothic. To my right, a skeleton in a wedding dress held an apple, a crescent moon cradling her background. To my right, a coffin floated down a river of black water; above was a sky full of stars and a falling comet.

Beyond, Shaya opened a door on a huge living room decorated in a New Age style. A huge elephant tapestry draped over a window. On a coffee table I saw an ashtray molded into the shape of two open hands. Two big couches, no television, an ottoman in the middle.

Alo walked to a wall with an incense stick poking from it. She lit it. Shaya plopped on the couch and took out a big bag of frosty oregano, followed by a small folder of thin white papers.

"She's not gone for good, kid. No one ever really is," Shaya said and proceeded to roll the greenery. "Sometimes space makes it better."

"I had no idea she lived around here. Her commute to school is terrible," I said, standing completely still by the door. "Is this your place?"

Shaya chuckled. "No one lives here."

Alo muttered to herself, but it sounded like Latin, possibly a chant. The incense smoke grew thicker. "Take a seat, kid. You want to see something cool?" She pointed to a book on the coffee table I hadn't noticed before.

"*The Tibetan Book of Living and Dying,*" I read the title aloud. Dog-eared were the pages when I opened it. Before I could finish a paragraph, another man entered the room dressed in bell-bottoms and a tight shirt, nearly a crop top, displaying his flattened stomach, a neatly picked Afro radiating around his face.

He plopped on the couch and kicked his feet up. "He a little old for a runaway," the new man said in a raspy voice, likely the result of smoking too many cigarettes. "I left the house at nine."

"Different times. This boy came prepared." Shaya laughed, strange-smelling smoke exiting his mouth. "Tents and shit."

"Ha, new times, old times." He gazed into my eyes. "A stolen car can be useful for a night's sleep. Especially if you got a Bonnie with you. Otherwise, chop shop, airbags, be good for a few days."

"My bread and butter," Shaya responded. "I'm running these days."

"Brown or white?" the other man asked.

"Whole rainbow."

"Show him." Alo gave Shaya a nudge.

Shaya took out a ziplock bag full of sugar, placed it on the table.

"Are you cooking something?" I asked, confused. Before Shaya answered a woman entered the living room, though I never heard the sound of a door opening or closing. She was wearing a bikini and flip-flops. In her hair were butterfly clips, and she had an eyebrow piercing.

"Who's the kid?" she asked in a sultry voice, too old for her age.

"New runaway," Alo answered for me. "Green."

"Never seen cocaine before?" The bikini woman chuckled.

"Indulging in drugs is dangerous," I exclaimed. They all went still, then slowly cracked smiles simultaneously.

"Having a soul is dangerous. Well, once you get one. Or earn one, rather," the bell-bottomed man replied.

"A soul isn't earned." I coughed from the smoke getting thicker in the room, like a blanket floating above.

"We're husks of DNA when we come out," Alo calmly stated, sitting on the couch near me. "A soul is earned through suffering and revelation. The entire essence of life itself. We're not saying you need LSD to do it, but . . ."

"A crash course, think of it that way." Shaya attempted to hand me the rolled oregano he was smoking. I put up my hand to reject it. "Fair enough. You're amongst good people. Your people. I can smell a lost soul for miles around." He sniffed the air, imitating a dog. "No harm will come to you, I promise."

"You have doors in your mind that cannot be opened through sobriety," the bikini woman expressed. "Unless you practice meditation daily, for years. Otherwise, ego death."

"Ego death?" I questioned, in awe of the string of words.

"A complete loss of subjective self-identity," Alo said. "Your ego got you here, but it will not travel with you into the great beyond. Suffering will hug you. Homelessness, despair. High highs."

"I'm not a lost soul," I pleaded. "I'm a distinct individual with high intelligence who lives in certain circumstances that force me to be tamed. Not that I want to be unhinged. But—"

"What's the point of being alive if you only feel it when you're close to death?" bell-bottoms jumped in.

"No, well, yes, in a way, I suppose," I said. "That might honestly be my whole reason for doing this. Basically, the higher my intelligence goes, the lower my happiness plummets. I cannot help that. And if I'm aware of this dilemma now, at the beginning of adolescence, then . . . excitement must be a part of my life. I need to feel . . ."

"He's starting to get it," the bikini woman said, reaching for the bag of sugar. "Which is why you need to remove yourself from yourself. Don't end up like me."

"Aside from your blatant disrespect for casual clothing and irresponsible drug abuse," I argued. "Not to mention, I have a high calculation that none of you exist within the means of a W-9, or any legal job for that manner. Still, judgment aside, I find you all tolerable, and enlightening." I was suddenly feeling a little hazy. I shook it off. "What happened to you?"

"I got so addicted to the feeling of being close to death that I died." Bikini woman smiled. She was missing a few teeth and the gaps in her mouth gave me a start.

"Not a bad send-off," bell-bottoms added. "A selfish life leads to a giving end. I learned that one. It seems unorthodox, kid. But everything in adulthood is a series of bewildering events. Sometimes, in my case, it was easier to take. Until the great beyond took me."

"Wow." Suddenly the haziness grew into relaxation. "I have no idea what you're talking about. I'm Ludwig, by the way."

"I'm not really here, by the way," bell-bottoms responded with a grin.

I laughed. "What?"

Alo and Shaya glanced at each other. "Kindred spirits, kid. We'll find you when you need us."

"What?" I repeated. I was having trouble focusing and the room began spinning. Faster and faster, all the colors blurring into one.

When I awoke I was outside on the curb, lying on a dirty white couch. The sun was piercing into my eyes. Across the street, with colorful graffiti behind them on the brick wall of an abandoned building, a few people were standing around a huge speaker. One of them climbed it and dangled his legs over the front.

A shock wave of punk music assaulted my body as I turned and twisted, trying to make sense of the previous night. I discovered cigarette butts and burn holes in the couch as I squirmed. While stretching my neck, I saw a teenager walking down the block holding a skateboard. He rapped lyrics out loud, as if casting a spell of protection over himself. As he passed by, he failed to acknowledge my existence.

I felt a strong desire to revisit the experience I'd had with another person. Give them the clues so they could give me perspective. My mother was the sole person I yearned for. I tugged on my bag, hearing the contents shift inside. Yet, when I tapped my pockets a familiar bulge, a crucial component, was missing. Before panic seeped deep into my skin, I sat up, checked once more. Confirmed. My cell phone was no longer there.

NATHANIEL

My little brother was a chess master at the age of seven years. By sixteen he had attained a perfect score on the SAT and started college a year early. By twenty-one, he embarrassed me by buying a better car. By twenty-two, he rose five levels in the field of his expertise. By twenty-six he proposed to a woman he'd only dated for five months. She rejected him, and he's been living alone for ten years. Now, he was standing next to me in Home Depot, because despite the fact he had been blessed with the intellect of a genius, he still had nothing better to do.

"Inexplicable, you say?" My little brother's mouth curved as he said it.

"Unexplainable. Everything was right there," I said, craning past the person in front of me to gauge how long it would take to get this key made.

"Maybe you did it yourself? Subconsciously, revisiting your past to help you with your present. Burying it won't work. I thought you would've known that. However, memory is a funny thing. It's seldom entirely accurate. If you tried to remember all the meals you had this week, I'm sure there would be several errors. It's a human brain condition. Or, on an easier level, perhaps . . . sleepwalking?"

My little brother got into the habit of solving other people's problems. He never understood the beauty of listening.

"I drink too much for that," I said. The smell of fresh-cut wood tickled my nose as I gave the line another look. "My coordination would land me in a ditch somewhere. Or curled up on the bathroom floor. The dog would've barked. Heather would've woken up. Shit, Ludwig? . . . Well, he sleeps hard. There was no evidence, no dirt, unearthing, nothing. Perfectly laid out, it was. Pristine."

"Hmm, maybe Satan is trying to teach you something?" the Younger One asked sarcastically.

"That's a stretch. We, neither of us, have been to church in over twenty years."

"But we agree it's some malevolent force?" my brother pressed.

I scowled. "Sure, fine. Dark forces."

"Better to name it. Easier to hypothesize. For definition's sake, let's call it 'The Devil's Work.'"

"Punishment for me taking a penny instead of leaving a penny?"

"You've done far worse," my brother reminded me.

"Once again . . ." I cleared my throat. "It was by accident."

"I looked for that mechanical dog toy for two weeks." My brother looked indignant. "I was heartbroken. You single-handedly ruined my Christmas."

"I broke it out of anger," I protested. "I didn't even know it was yours."

"Mom made up for it."

"Can we focus here?" I asked, turning to face him.

The Younger One shrugged. "Hard to not be nostalgic when I'm in your presence, Older One."

"Because you're a hermit. Sunlight, a beer, and a strip club would do you good." I paused. "I guess it helps your writing though. You're light-years ahead of me."

"Women are to be treasured, not bought," my brother said philosophically. Considering he hadn't been laid in almost a decade, I wondered if he was putting them on an unreachable pedestal.

"Chance," I said to him," can we at least talk about the urn?"

"I'm surprised you stole it."

"Twice again, you didn't fucking want it." The line finally shifted up. We were two people away from the checkout. I controlled my anger and lowered my voice. "You didn't go to the funeral."

My brother met my eyes calmly. "He really was Satan."

I opened my mouth and closed it again. "You're remembering it wrong," I finally said.

Next in line.

"The backyard is one thing, but where did this key come from?" I pondered, wiggling it in my brother's face. "It wasn't in the urn when I got it. And I never buried it. I put it in the attic somewhere."

"Hmm, better in the basement," my brother said. "Closer to hell."

The locksmith leaned forward and took the key from my hand delicately. Behind his company apron and orange shirt his whimsical flowing white hair flowed, a grandfather's body, reading glasses hanging around his neck by a chain.

"A skeleton key. Otherwise known as a passkey, or master key. One fifty," he said.

The low price took importance from the evil supernatural forces at bay. A blowback to reality.

"Let me have five," I said.

While walking to the car I momentarily looked up at the big aquamarine sky. Internally, I prayed for a sign. Externally, I handed Chance a key. With great reluctance, he stuffed it in his pocket.

"I'm not involved with this," he said haughtily. "All my skeletons live on the surface. I sleep with them every night. There's no chest, or locks, or secret doors to be opened. It's a fool's journey."

"I'm going to give one to Heather too," I said.

"As . . . uh, special as she is, I'm sure she'll travel that paved road of confusion with you. I mean, she has for how long now?" my brother asked.

"I forget."

I approached the front door of my house. A sensation ran down my arms. I grabbed the master key, shoved it in the door. After a gentle twist, I removed it. Prancing around the living room, encircled in a trail of smoke from a piece of burning sage, Heather glanced at me. Her eyes sent me a telepathic message: *Leave me alone and I'll leave you alone.* I nodded, left her copy of the master key on the coffee table, and continued on.

Whatever glass laying between us had begun to show cracks. We were reverting to our younger selves. The minutiae of everyday chores, the monotony of standard responses, all seemed to fade slowly. We saw each other again as individuals. Not parents, nor partners in a life race. All it took was sex and silence.

In my study I destroyed the area by moving shelves, knocking over stands, searching and testing every lock imaginable. Defeated, I sat in the chair, powered on the computer, and took out a small bottle of unopened vodka. Before twisting the cap and hearing its sweet scrunch, I brought it closer to my face. Right on the label, plain as day, was a symbol of a lock: the company's logo.

My sanity tested, I grabbed the master key and put it next to the bottle. I pressed forward. The key went inside. I turned it and the entire logo turned with it to the right. The vodka inside bubbled. I twisted the key back and, now dry, out it came. I sniffed the contents; no sting to my nostrils. I carefully touched it on my lips and licked. It was water.

HEATHER

I dreaded the noon call coming my way. Smudging, meditation, and a glass of wine still wouldn't hold up against the supreme power of my mother. Lying worked for a while. A text back, something ambiguous: I was busy working, let me call you later. Through the years, realizing what little time both of us have left, being dishonest didn't serve my spirit anymore.

Head-on, I would go into the pyre with eyes open, inhaling the smoke. It wasn't that we had a turbulent relationship; the problem lived in our inability to see the other person's side. Every conversation ended with me conceding. Five minutes until noon, I grabbed my comfort food: a small bottle of Pepsi and a honey bun. I yelled for Nathaniel twice, making sure he yelled back. I could tell from the projection of the sound what room he was in. If needed, I'd make him my distraction to get off the phone. Normally, it'd be Ludwig. The phone rang.

"Afternoon, Heather. How's the family?" My mother's been answering the phone with that same question since even before I was married with kids. Estranged, she was. The black sheep through two generations.

"Good, good. Ludwig's out with his friend. Nathaniel's just hanging out in the house."

"Out? Now? Well, if he catches it, he might be all right. It only affects the old from what I hear."

"What only affects the old?" I asked.

"That virus from China. Corona," my mother answered. "It's making its way across the world, darling. If it keeps up, we might not see each other for months."

How amazing would that be? I thought.

"A friend from work mentioned it," I said. "I'm not too worried. At least for now. He needs to hang out with his friends. More and more, actually. Get a social life. I ended the tutoring. Ms. Cumberbatch hasn't returned my calls, and I never searched for a replacement."

"Ludwig hated that woman," my mother said dismissively. "Said she smelled like cabbage, with the personality of a scorpion. She might be dead, dear."

"Don't say that."

"She was born in what, '55? Always had that persistent whooping cough. Longer than ten days too. I'm seven years older, and when's the last time you heard me cough?"

I thought for a moment. "Off the top of my head, maybe, Christmas?"

"That was a regular cough," my mother corrected me. "You've got to listen to the nuance in the sound. There was no phlegm. Anyway, I had a dream last night about Dr. Morgan. Do you remember her?"

"Yes. My god, it's been a long time. Every time I hear Bob Marley, I think about her."

"She took a shine to you. After you went through"— my mother paused deliberately—"that little thing in college."

The hand that wasn't holding the phone closed into a fist, my nails digging into my palm. "It wasn't a thing. Don't make it sound small and passive. Call it what it is."

"Therein lies the problem, darling," my mother said, sounding infuriatingly calm. "I don't know what to call it. All I know is that you stopped taking your pills and wouldn't listen to a single word I said. I gave up after a few years. Figured you were crazy like me. We're cursed, you know."

"It was a major depressive episode, Mom." I spat out the words. "That's what it was. I didn't need pills. I just needed some time, and I've been fine ever since."

"See, time. That's what you call it."

"I know my own mind, Mom." I raised my voice to emphasize my point.

"See? Dr. Morgan called it early signs of schizophrenia." I could feel a headache building as she continued to talk. "Now, I know you hate when I bring this up; I just wanted to congratulate you. Not many people lead normal lives with that condition. Remember that famous mathematician who had it? He did fine for some years, until the 5150."

"She's wrong." I felt the panic in my voice and forced it down. Rose appeared behind me and placed her hand on my shoulder.

"Oh dear." My mother sighed. "I've upset you again. Can I at least tell you what she told me in the dream?"

"It doesn't matter," I retorted. "That's your mind speaking through her. It won't change what I went through, and it won't change the fact that you never listened or believed your own daughter. This is why we don't talk often."

"It's your word versus a doctor, darling. A trained professional. I mean, if it were Ludwig, who would you believe? I know you don't want it to be true. But you've always lied to me. Your word became less credible. And, in the dream—"

"I have to go," I dissembled. "Nathaniel needs me to help with something in the backyard. I think the dog buried his watch."

"Wait, before you go . . ." My mother's voice stopped me from hanging up. "The real reason I called is that it's my birthday."

I took the phone away from my ear to see the Facebook notification. Probably why the sage burned so strangely. My mother continued.

"Heather, were you going to call me at all today?"

"Yes," I said automatically, "right after I finished up some work."

"Another lie."

"Mother, I've got to go."

Rose took the phone from me and hung it up. I stumbled back to the couch, drank some of the soda. I remembered the last time I communicated with Dr. Morgan. It was in the library, the same day I met Nathaniel for the first time. Right before I had looked at my transcript I sent her a message, saying I wouldn't be needing her assistance any longer. Like when only a few minutes ago I used Nathaniel for an escape, which back then had turned into a pregnancy. Had I not read the diagnosis, had I not rejected it, I wonder where I would be now? I was just sad, and only for a year, which is normal for most college kids.

Rose whispered in my ear, *et non sunt normalis.*

I texted the Wilsons and canceled the gathering we'd planned for tonight. They were a nice couple, younger, eager to play games that spanned fifty years in use. Nathaniel and I fed off their vigor. But the reunion with my mother via telephone had ruined the social need inside me. I yearned for the ground to open and swallow me whole. To shield me from the mounting eruption of memory and pain and buried information. After my stomach began to rumble from the junk food I'd forced into it, I grabbed Nathaniel's strange skeleton key, running my fingers over the groove.

There was some commotion in the study, but I dragged my feet past it, up the stairs, and lay in bed. Staring at the ceiling, holding the key, a thought crossed my mind. I opened the closet, pushed past my collection of shoes gathered over the years, and grabbed a heart-shaped box.

A decade before, I lost the key to it. So, I took Nathaniel's, inserted it in the lock, and turned. The box creaked open.

All the papers had Dr. Morgan's signature on them, along with mine. I obtained the information from a boy I dated before Nathaniel. He was a hacker who owed me a favor. A diagnosis was written on the top page:

> *The patient consistently speaks of Rose. An imaginary friend that's followed her since childhood. A sign of coping? Strong imagination? However, voices, and seeing things that aren't there? The wicker chair, the Tibetan sound bowl, clear signs of hallucinations, or psychosis. Underlying mental condition. Possibly link to sch—*

I folded the paper at first, then crumbled it in my hands. Before I let emotion overtake I yelled Nathaniel's name, but he didn't answer. I started to close the box, but stopped and stared at the wood-carved heart in the lid. It was painted purple. Suddenly, it began to glow. Vibrantly, stronger and stronger, with a pulse that matched my own. Terrified, I put the key inside the box and closed it.

LUDWIG

Back door. The back door is always open, that's what she said. Each step brought a kaleidoscope of fragments from my experience the night before. A skeleton in a wedding dress holding an apple. The crescent moon cradling her background. I dodged the overgrown weeds and broken glass in the backyard of the shanty house. *Focus*, I told myself, as my heartbeat matched the rhythm of Calypso maracas. All logic exited the shell of my frame. Panic ruled my five senses. The back door, she said, I repeated in my head.

Foaming at the mouth, shielded by a gate, two rabid dogs barked at me when I neared. A blue light went on in the kitchen, muted by deep purple shades. My knees dropped inches from the concrete steps and I squatted myself back to an upright position. One of the dogs leaped at the gate as the door swung open.

In azure shorts, her tan thighs exposed, more pronounced than I had imagined, wearing a thin white shirt, Angel stepped before me. A sliver of sunlight was captured in her brown eyes, and while temporarily blinded, I saw a savior, quickly followed by a hellcat, then finally a three-headed siren. When sight was given back to her, I pointed my finger at her and exclaimed, "You stole my phone!"

"How do you know it was me? Besides, I took it for insurance," she replied slyly while grinning at the dogs, who sat politely in her presence.

"I need it. I've changed . . . ah, I've reconceived my mission. Certain events have . . . taken place." The words fought each other coming out my mouth, hurdling over and past one another.

"You left me," Angel replied sotto voce.

"That's not how I remember it. The phone!" I stuck out my hand.

"You're welcome." She took my phone out of her back pocket casually. "I left mementos. Images meant to last."

"They'll be deleted promptly. Now, please!"

"Come inside. Please."

I about-faced and the two dogs snarled at me, all forty-two teeth on display. Admitting defeat, I walked with my back toward her, testing each step with my toes. Never letting my gaze leave the mongrels.

"Bark Twain and Prince of Barkness, meet Salvador Dogi," she whispered behind me.

"I'm not a dog. I'm a teenage boy. A slightly racked, neurotic, and out-of-balance boy," I said, getting closer.

I felt her hands touch my hips, draw me closer. In the comfort of her embrace, her thinly clothed breasts against my back, my knees began to buckle. The two dogs laid down in the brown grass. My newly found libido and massive brain began a game of chess. As she blew on my neck, I simultaneously felt a shiver run down my back as I tried to hold myself in check.

"Are there rations in this fleabox?" I inquired.

"Army grade." She spun me around and steered me inside the house.

When I closed the door, sealing myself in the dragon's lair, above the window I noticed a poster of two army men interrogating a civilian. The words *MK-Ultra* were written above it. In my peripheral vision I noted piles of dishes lying in the sink. Scattered messes on the countertop. There was a rug below my feet with random damp spots.

Now face to face, I observed her symmetry. The retroussé nose, fat cheeks, curved lips, the sweet scent of candy on her breath. A brief tennis match in our eyes. I blinked, then blanked, momentarily.

"Take off your clothes," she said.

I blinked again in surprise. "Why?"

"You don't smell yourself like I do. There is a cloud of dank living on you. Did they drug you? The two weirdos?"

"Drugs?" I started to shake my head. "No, wait." I looked away to gather my thoughts. "There was drugs."

"You mean there *were* drugs."

"What?"

"Who provided the drugs?" Angel demanded.

"The two vagabonds. Alo and Shaya, and their friends. The woman . . . in the bikini. All of them."

"You got high with a woman in a bikini? Good job, Salva—"

"Who may or may not have been deceased. Is 'have been' correct? Perfect present tense verb," I began mumbling to myself, reigniting my intelligence.

"Why?" she responded, genuinely shocked.

"What do you mean why? Because of the mortal clock. It's in the book."

"Slow down."

"*The Tibetan Book of the Dead and Dying*, and the conversation, and the pictures. The pictures on the wall." My vision went a bit dizzy. "I'm overstimulated."

Angel chuckled. "Welcome to my life."

"This has nothing to do with you."

She took a step closer and our noses touched. "It does. It always does."

"You're just blurring my vision." I backed away, even though my spirit said not to. "Phone first. Games later."

"Deal."

Suddenly, heavy footsteps from above brought loud creaks above my head. As if the wooden planks, bricks, and walls of the house recognized my presence. An intruder. I heard a few bones pop from a hard stretch.

Angel's eyes went wide, and she tried to push me back toward the exit door.

"Don't touch me," I yelled.

"Who is in my sanctuary?" A mighty roar came from an unseen woman, whose voice rattled the bones in my body. "Angel!"

All the dread I felt transported to Angel, and, for a glorious moment, I watched her shift out of her element.

"Yes, Agnes?"

"Answer me, girl." An overweight woman with bushy eyebrows reared her monstrous head around the corner. "This child may be infected. He's sullied the entire home," she barked, coming into full view. She was draped in a large flowy dress decorated in sunflowers. A beast of two chins.

"He just forgot his phone, at school, and came to get it," Angel struggled to reply.

"That's even worse! You know how many hands touch a cell phone daily?"

Internally, I tried to calculate a formula for that equation. However, Agnes gripped Angel's shoulders with flames in her eyes. She clawed my phone from her possession, backed away, and placed it on a table littered in ash. Then she opened a drawer and retrieved a rusted hammer with a red rubber grip. Petrified, I lost my voice to speak. In reaction, I just threw my hands up. Angel squinted. Her face distorted.

"And it's on 5G—that's how it spreads! You know that! I've told you that several times! 5G!" She proceeded to bash the phone with ungodly strength, shattering each piece of glass, screw, frame, and circuit.

NATHANIEL

Fifteen years ago. I held the two tests that Heather had just peed on. I read the results three times, expecting the words to change. A stolen car, blaring music, was speeding down the street. I heard the rumble of thunder in the sky. There was a stain of liquor on the carpet from a bottle I had spilled the night before.

Heather's eyes bubbled with tears. In time, mine did the same. She placed my hand on her stomach.

"We're having a sage," she said confidently.

"With a pig's tail."

"Like *One Hundred Years of Solitude.*"

"I guess that only applies if we're brother and sister," I commented.

"Or aunt and nephew. Well, in this case, uncle and niece."

"We should stop talking about incest."

"I'm happy." Heather stroked her stomach. "Rose told me this would happen. That this weekend would be it."

"I'm the only one you've told, right?"

"About the baby?" she asked.

"No, about Rose," I said.

"My mother . . ." Heather admitted. "Who, in all honestly, I wouldn't care to tell anything else."

"Good."

As she proceeded to travel down the rabbit hole of first trimesters, bananas, and high-waisted stretchy pants, I poured myself a drink. I never confronted Heather about Rose. Parts of me believed it to be a phase. I knew about the dark nights. The knives she said whispered to her in her dreams. Overlooked, a miscalculation on my side, I supposed. She'd never hurt me, that much was true. Herself, that was questionable. It was my fatal flaw that forced me to ignore all the signs. I loved her.

The first person I told, after about two weeks, was my little brother. Heather slept twice as much, leaving me to wallow in my free time. Deep in my study, finishing a chapter to a story that would never be read by another pair of eyes, I called him.

"Birth order, that's important. You're going to have another, I imagine?" my little brother asked.

"I'm not thinking that far ahead," I said. "You know me. You know I don't foresee shit."

"Well, that opens the possibilities of an only child syndrome. But if another arrives, your first will have a slightly higher IQ."

"That's bullshit," I argued. "You're the family genius."

"It is not. Read *Born to Rebel* by psychologist Frank J. Sulloway. In fact, you need to read a few books. For preparation, of course. I can provide you with about thirty, merely for pleasure."

I scowled. "You hate me, right?"

"Down to the core." My brother smiled.

"Then if you hate me, please turn off your brain. Just listen to me. A child isn't a problem to be solved."

My younger brother paused. "I . . . I'm listening."

"Say 'Congratulations.' Tell me all the shit people want to hear in this situation. Support me."

Younger One sighed. "Against all logical thought. I say to you, Nathaniel Falcon, you're going to be the shittiest father in the world. The court will develop a new system named after you called 'The Nathaniel Law.' Whereas, any future fathers who display such a lack of parenting skills, and complete disdain for human life, be hogtied and catapulted into the nearest body of water at dawn on the first day of autumn. Heather will realize that you are more beast than man, and never leave you, but will poison your meals and drinks every day for twenty-five years. Her weapon of choice will be anti-freeze. Your child will literally be half anti-Christ, half lizard-person, and will hypnotize the world into an apocalyptic state, whereas aliens won't even bother colonizing us because we have destroyed the planet."

"Thank you, Chance." My heart swelled from the loving words.

"Now, on a serious note. Can we talk about sci-fi fan fiction now?"

That same night, in a drunken stupor, I went digging in the attic. Old items, packed away to die. In a box within a box I located a small mandolin. All the strings missing, bad internal damage, machine heads broken off. A long scratch across the top. It reminded me of keg stands, mushrooms, riots, and unwarranted, random sex. My band's name, nights of jamming in my friend's basement until morning. Belief in a flat earth. A subscription to the nonsensical message "*Anything is possible.*" The person I used to be. My life before twenty-five.

"I'm never going play again," I mumbled to myself.

In the backyard, near a bed of roses, where I planned to install my next group of plants, I sank the shovel into the dirt. Each dig shed weight off my past. Vigorously, I dug a hole two times the size of the mandolin. Tossing it in like a corpse, I stared at the hole.

"What else can I put in the ground?" I asked myself.

Current day. The mandolin stared back at me, leaning against a wall. Mocking me. Reminding me that I was once an artist. After picking it up, I stuck my hand inside the hole and took out a folded piece of paper. Alexandria's phone number scribbled in pen, still legible. The friend I would reconnect with. Someone who excelled in life and became a lawyer. Someone I would find at a common place of loneliness. My only tryst.

Neatly, I put the paper in my pocket and kept searching through Nate's discarded items. Up next, a journal from high school. All the pages stiff and curved from water damage. Each entry about my father. The distance between us an ocean of misunderstanding. Throughout his life and mine, we never knew each other. A sudden sharp pain brought an image of Ludwig. I closed the book. This would go back underground.

Childhood trauma began to attack me, unleashing itself all at once. I reached for the vodka bottle and swigged as hard as I could, nearly drowning myself in . . . water. Ten minutes later, with my hand against the tiled part of the wall, pants down to my ankles, I cascaded a bladder's worth of liquid. A purging. Eruptions began bubbling below. I kneeled from pressure building itself up and out. Not a drop of vomit. A gold object, protruding from my mouth. Painfully, I reached with my hand. With my peripheral I scanned the bathroom twice, expecting Heather to burst inside. Catching me in a complete moment of what-the-fuckness.

I pulled harder, and tears streamed down my face. When the object finally came out, I stared at it for a solid thirty seconds. There, in the center of my hand, covered in saliva, was a silver master key. Another one. But how? I gave away the copies, purposely. Why would I have two? At this point, I dropped all charades.

"Heather!" I yelled out, like a child to its mother. "Baby!"

No response. More panic. I screamed again. Nothing. I escaped the bathroom. Too quickly, with my name-brand slides on, I missed a step. My feet attempted to conquer each other, one over the other. I crashed down on the hardwood floor. My vision went black, and I slipped into a dream.

HEATHER

Without checking in, no conversation had, I stormed to my car, got in, and turned it on so angrily the engine cried. After releasing the key, hearing the car steady itself, I rested my cheek on the steering wheel and whispered apologies to my vehicle.

While in reverse, I didn't acknowledge my textbook neighbors vying for my attention. The sweet, unscathed Wilsons. Two blocks down, going about 10 mph over the speed limit, stuck at a red light, I checked my phone. I had never hit *send* on the text. The Wilsons didn't know I had canceled. And now, for some inexplicable reason, they had arrived five hours earlier than expected.

I cleared my head of it and gazed at the Texas-style home on the corner. My imagination was nowhere to be found. All I could fathom was a chandelier made of antlers. I noticed the light had turned green and I sped through. The melodies emanating from the speakers brought a fading peace to my anger, quelling every three minutes. I switched radio stations feverishly. Anything to soothe: Christmas songs, smooth jazz, and country music all proved inadequate. For the rest of the ride, I sat in silence and brewing rage.

When I entered the hospital, the abundance of nurses matched the overwhelming smell of mothballs. There were families in line waiting to speak with the receptionist. During my wait time, I soaked in all the details of the building. The dull colors of the walls. The disregard for speed, speech, and the present. All of my nails were bitten down to nubs when I finally came into full view of the receptionist. From behind the thick screen of Plexiglas, I grabbed her attention.

"Who you here to see?" she asked lackadaisically.

"Lani."

Both her eyebrows arched simultaneously. "Lani got a last name? I got about three of them in here."

"Lani Tyler."

"There we go. You help me, I help you. Lani Tyler." She slammed a large binder on the desk before her. I winced, watching her lick her thumb unnecessarily.

Flying through the pages, she stopped with incredible accuracy. Years of doing the same thing over and over, robotic. "Fifth floor, room 508. Your first time here?"

"No."

"You sure?" She leaned toward me. "I've seen every face of every visitor since 1978. And you look extremely unfamiliar."

"I was much younger. Maybe even shorter? Hair was braided at the time. Wearing a—"

"A stupid college shirt. That obnoxious gray with just the words 'college' in black. Yea, now I remember you."

She printed out a visitor sticker, removed the back covering, and spread it on my shirt. "If she's not there, she might be in the game room. Which is the fourth floor, right in the lobby."

"She still plays?" I asked, with a touch of surprise in my words.

"Five times a day. No one has beat her since 1999."

A series of clanks diverted my attention as the numbers scrolled the elevator's ascent. Fifth floor. The doors parted. My first step sent a wave of remorse from my toes to my brain. As I waltzed through all the pent-up rage subsided, and when I saw the empty bedroom in room 508, I about-faced.

Fourth floor. In a true reveal, soon I saw the game room/lobby. A frail woman, her long silver hair braided, drooping to one side, rested in a wheelchair, smiling hard. My mother's eyes lit up. She stretched her neck to see me over the head of her opponent. I approached their chessboard bashfully, pulled up a chair, and nodded.

She nodded back and returned to the game. Her opponent held a grim face, struggling to think, looking at the coordinates of the pieces, calculating an exit strategy.

"Fried Liver Attack. Goddamnit!" The woman banged on the table. All the pieces lifted and fell back in their correct upright position.

"You don't use the Sicilian right, darling," my mother responded in jest, before killing the rook with her knight. "You must learn the theory before throwing the game pieces around. I have some books to help you on the subject. Heather." She arched her head toward me. "What do you see here?"

Out of turn, Mom moved a pawn forward one space. Her smile widened as I pondered what the point was.

"You moved a piece one square," I answered hastily, feeling strange pressure.

"What about you, Margret?" my mother asked.

"Besides you going out of turn, you backed up the bishop, because it was left unattended."

"Ah, and I see, e4 to e5. So . . ." She turned back to me. "It's okay for us to see things differently, as long as we all see the same thing."

Back in her room, beneath a triptych interpretation of *Starry Night* by van Gogh, I lifted her from the wheelchair to the hospital bed. Rather gracelessly, I rolled her onto it; she swayed left and right before settling in the middle.

"Like a roller coaster. Is this my present?" There was love in her voice.

"I didn't have time to pick something up."

"Keep lying, darling. It keeps your teeth white."

I rubbed my hands together awkwardly before apologizing. "You know I love you."

"Do I? I know you love the idea of me. The idea of being a black woman whose parents stayed together her whole life. It's an achievement all on its own. Makes your story better." She sighed and I spoke again.

"Dr. Morgan was going to put me on pills. Is that what you wanted? I would've turned out maladjusted and drugged. It even prevents orgasms. That's the life you wanted for me. So, I ran off with Nathaniel. Made my own route at the fork in the road. He accepts me."

"He is a man." My mother waved a dismissive hand. "His entire life will be accepting any woman who spreads for him."

"It's more than that."

"Correct. Bravery." A slight smile tugged at her lips. "I like that in you. I like how you made your own paths in life. However, as I have come to realize in the passing of time, there's nothing more dangerous than believing your own lies. The story you tell yourself over and over. It will eat you in the end. I don't want that for you. Sometimes, I think it's the only reason God keeps me around. I didn't want it for your father either. If you're going to tell anyone on this planet, let it be me. I keep secrets; you know that."

"Tell you what?"

She sighed deeply. "Tell me the truth, Heather."

"So, I have an overactive imagination. I daydream. I—"

"—see things," she finished.

"Rose isn't a thing; she's just a friend," I protested. "A friend in my head. That's normal."

"For children, but even then it's questionable. It's okay to be flawed. All the best people are."

"I'm fine, honestly. My life isn't perfect, but I don't feel crazy. I'm not a danger to myself or others. I don't have wild mood swings. I'm balanced with Rose."

"Then the best gift you could give me would be to leave her in the past," my mother said. "Prove to me that she's a creation of your 'overactive imagination' and not a sign."

"A sign of schizophrenia." The words fell heavily out of my mouth. "That's impossible."

"Tell me you don't see her right now."

Out of the corner of my eye, Rose floated through the large windows and landed gracefully in the room. Her hair defied gravity, and all the skin on her face was undulating.

"Tell me you're in control," my mother said.

LUDWIG

Agnes's laugh reverberated off the walls of the 19th-century home. On the floor above, separated by a closed door and a hallway, I felt Angel's presence on the other side. Her beldame aunt watched TV comedy on mute, reading the subtitles.

The house was always kept dark. Agnes fully subscribed to the conspiracy that all planned obsolescence started with the light bulb in the 1920s. Manufacturers deliberately shortened the life of their products to increase demand. Whether I believed it or not held no weight in the gravity of our situation.

"NOO, DON'T GO IN THE BASEMENT," Agnes screamed, before slapping her knee and entering yet another laugh-fest, complete with snorts.

In between the laughs, catching seconds of time, I tapped the door in sequence. Five minutes went by. No sound, except the floorboards bending to the weight and will of Agnes as she walked to the kitchen and back to the living room.

Another burst of boisterous laughter. Angel tapped back. What we both knew: Agnes sleeps when her body can no longer stay awake. In her mind, the cost of losing consciousness was astronomical. She'd be vulnerable.

She was also a coffee addict, to combat the natural tiredness of the human body. Earlier, during the slaughter of our smartphones, Angel slipped out whatever she could to help us, thinking ahead. Our only salvation was an old butter knife, russet-colored.

Another burst of laughter occurred, and before I could send a new Morse code message Angel slid the knife through the space beneath her door. I watched the handle appear beneath my own. For the next hour, mercilessly, I worked the lock on my door. When the sweet relief of snoring was made audible from below, I quietly opened my door and began working on Angel's.

Two hours later, we were free. She embraced me in the quiet, and due to the short-lived trauma we both had experienced, I hugged her back. From then on, we communicated only in sign language, although it took a few minutes for our eyes to adjust to the dark.

"Who keeps doors with the inside locked?" I asked.

"She believes people cannot be trusted," Angel replied.

"What's the plan? We creep out the same door we had entered?"

"No go." Angel shook her head. "It requires a key. Every door in this house does."

"We can pick it."

"Wrong again. It's a smart lock."

"Where's her phone?" I asked.

"No one knows." Angel shrugged.

"How do you get in and out?"

"She allows me to," Angel answered. "That's how I ran away the first time."

"Tragic."

"Olive juice," she said, gesturing wisely.

"What?" I made the symbol sternly with my hand.

"You don't get it?"

"We're going to poison her with olive juice?" I was still lost. "Where is it?"

"No." Angel rolled her eyes. "Mouth it out," she whispered.

"How does one mouth out sign language?"

"How are we arguing this way?" She raised an eyebrow. "It's impressive."

"Should've just given me my phone," I muttered.

Angel smiled. "You olive juice me too."

"Stop with the juice," I ordered. "Think."

"I've olive juiced you for so long." Angel moved closer to me.

I tried to find the sign language equivalent of "Jesus" but couldn't figure it out.

We monitored our footfalls as we got closer to the beast. I took a step with every snore. Angel made her way to the front door, monitoring it, looking for a keypad or switch. I had my own agenda and wandered into the kitchen. I heard Angel tinkering too loudly but disregarded it. My plan B was perfect.

I found my object. I carefully approached Agnes from behind, then I raised it. Angel turned to me, her mouth a huge O and wide open eyes.

"Ludwig!" she shouted, as I brought down a frying pan straight into Agnes's face. "What are you doing?"

"She'll sleep longer this way. It's science."

"Ludwig!" She shouted my name again and pushed me. I dropped the frying pan accidentally. It landed on Agnes's face again and we heard a crunch. "What if she's dead? She's still my aunt." Her eyes watered. "This is the stupidest thing you've ever done!"

"Hear me out," I said. "All you need to do is hit a person hard enough that their brain goes thirty-five miles per hour. It will overtake the speed of the cerebrospinal fluid. It prevents brain injury."

"That causes brain injury!" she protested.

I hadn't considered that. "Well, I'm not thinking straight, obviously!"

"None of this would've happened if—"

A phone rang. A landline. We went quiet. It rang six times. Agnes never moved, but there was wheezing to her breathing now. I felt the fire from Angel's eyes. Symbolically, it lit up the room. Except, the amount of indifference I had built up halted any recognition of it. An answering machine went off. We heard the message.

"Agnes, it's Bubby. Before you say it, yes, I'm still working with him. Good kid. Small balls, grapes really, but a good kid. There's a lot of small-ball men in this town. Sixteen, seventeen maybe? That ain't a lot, is it? Well, you know how my math goes. In one ear, out my asshole. He's a terrible detective, but who's still in this besides us? Anyhoo, I can't tell what time it is because the whiskey's got me stuck on the floor. And my damn sundial tipped over, stuck at noon for some reason. When you get a chance, dial nine-one, then when I call back hit one again. But don't hang up on the other line. Just ignore it, press one, then give them my address. For all I know, whiskey might've been poison. It was payment for our last case. Wait . . . I hear something. Never mind. Next-door neighbor's dog is barking at the wind. Or he's fucking his wife. Ha, you'll laugh at that when you hear this. Okay, don't forget—nine, then one. I'll call you back."

NATHANIEL

I awoke inside the dream. Standing on a roof made of limestone, I attempted to transpose the strange markings on the cave walls. There was a tear in my suit. I fingered the hole, tracing the seams up to my shoulder patch. Nova Corp. A violent cough erupted inside me. When I opened my mouth, a black fluid drifted out and away from my face toward the entrance. Behind a blazing wall of light, tall, thin figures with enormous heads entered.

Visible veins showed all over their pates, a tiny, blinking electrode traveling through the highways of each. I watched their skulls pulsate with thoughts. The one closest to me sent messages into my brain, deep into my subconscious.

I felt peace. Its skin transitioned from teal to black to cherry red in succession. Its neck was two feet long. Its elongated alienfingers began to glow, and as it twisted its hand, I found my equilibrium shifting back to that on Earth. It forced me right-side-up. Now standing on my own will, the aliens knelt to me. In awe, I tried to speak but found myself mute. As if I'd lost the use of my tongue.

They escorted me through the blinding light, which led, unraveling, to a thriving metropolis. The cave I'd been in seemed to be an exhibit in their city square. Millions of confetti particles floated upward when I took my first step on a road made of glass. Thousands of them bowed to me. I heard a series of clicks and grunts in concert. They were greeting me. Celebrating me.

"What is this place?" I asked subliminally.

The first one I'd made contact with stared at my head. Then, as its head began pulsating, I received a clear telepathic message.

"Lord of lords," it managed to say.

I waswhisked away in a floating apparatus that traveled sideways and upwards through the magnificent city. I witnessed flora and fauna unnatural to human eyes. Skyscrapers that kissed the greenish-purplish clouds above. We arrived at a terrace made of solid gold that turned silver when touched under pressure. Inside a room made of glass, my clothes were taken off, and I was dressed in silk garbs. The one from the cave placed its face into mine and its skin flattened to transform into a mirror.

"Is this acceptable?" it said to me.

"I don't understand," I replied.

"Lords of lords don't have time for understanding. Only ordainment."

"My ship crashed here by mistake. I was headed to Venus-9."

"You are on Venus-9."

The planet moved for me, placing me before a giant throne made of water. Hesitantly, I touched it; ripples traversed it and when I pressed, my throne was firm. I sat down. It spun over. Before me, thousands of aliens a hundred feet below were looking up at me on bended knees. The concert of clicks and grunts grew louder, harmonious, like a communal prayer.

"You are ready," my escort said.

Above me, a floating piece of concrete lowered itself into my view. Bound in chains, beaten, bloodied, also on his knees, my father, except he was my age, opened one eye, and was staring into my soul. Placed in the center of his forehead is a keyhole.

"The ceremonial sacrifice is at hand!" the escort communicates to the subjects below.

I felt their adoration in my bones. They loved me. The escort knelt one last time. Floating about his pulsating skull was the silver master key. I grabbed it as the throne extended itself toward the floating piece of concrete. I stoodto a wave of cheers. This time it was in English.

"Slay the wretched! Slay the unclean!" the escort yelled behind me.

With each step my father's features morphed into my own. Inches away, he has become me. I stared down at myself. I placed the key at the base of the keyhole, but didn't slip it in right away. The other me closed his eyes.

"Slay us . . . remove the unclean."

I pushed the key in. Turned the lock. An implosion occurred in my body. I was transported into the other me. Drenched in liquid silver, I watched the original version of myself turn his back, raise his hands. More confetti rose from below.

My childhood rage yelled for freedom.

"Noooo! It's not me! I'm not me!" I screamed in English.

"The Devil has been purified," the escort announced.

"That's not who I am! I am no Lord."

"This world is your world. A world that lives in your mind." It was Heather's voice, from a place unknown.

"Heather? Please!" I pleaded.

"It is okay to be flawed."

"Save me from myself! I need you!" I cried the words like a child. "And I will save you."

"But I am broken . . . as you have said. My reality is through stained glass. I am unclean."

"We are the same! I feel things that aren't there. I walk through shadows in the day! I am a husk within a husk. Bring me to you! You are the only one who can do it!"

"What's the magic word?"

My eyes opened. I saw the ceiling of my house. Out of focus, I watched Heather's face come into view slowly. She resembled God. I could see her mouth moving, but the sound in my ears was like waves crashing on the beach. Feeling returned to my hands. I wrapped them around her neck and pulled her close to me.

"I love you."

HEATHER

I watched him ramble, staring at the bald spot in the center of his head as he held my knees, crying into my shirt, wetting it below my navel. He spoke so incoherently. I caught only every third word he spoke.

"Two pieces fit . . . the gap of . . . Nova Corp story . . ." he slurred.

Cradling him like a baby in my arms, I used my mother's voice on him.

"Do you want to go to the hospital? Are you in any pain, Nate?"

He looked at me when I spoke his name. As if it was a code word for decoding the universe. He stood up, kissed me like I was another woman, hugged me, and simply walked away. With his back toward me, he said, "I'm okay."

Stealthily, I stalked his movements. His study was filled to the brim, objects splayed all around. I spied him sitting down, turning on the computer. On cue, backing away, I made my way to the bedroom. I opened the closet, got on my knees, and revisited the heart-shaped box. Once in my possession, I wandered to the backyard and noticed the shovel resting on the gate.

Sitting in a wicker chair to my left, Rose glared at me, then to the shovel.

"You're better than him," she said in English.

In the unoccupied seat parallel to her, I sat. Both of us gazed at the shovel. "I miss my son."

"Which one?"

"Nathaniel is not my child. Well, Nate, rather. He's just changing. Like . . . me."

"Like your mother?"

"To be honest . . ." I briefly moved to one of Nathaniel's stash spots, one he didn't know I was aware of. I took out a cigarette, sparked it with a match. "She's never changed. From my earliest memory until now. Same woman."

"She doesn't know you as I do."

I exhaled. "Maybe I don't know myself? Maybe that's why I'm always drifting off? Lying." I took in another long pull. "Does it stop, Rose?"

"The exploration of who one is never ceases until the person expires. Every day you are someone new."

"I meant this," I said, pointing at nothing in particular. "This game."

"You are playing chess against yourself. I am merely the board. The pieces."

The cigarette burned down. I sparked another one. "If I grab that shovel. Bury that box. Will you go away?"

"Look what happened to Nate."

I heard the words, but she was no longer visible. Suddenly, there was a rustling in the grass. The top of Cliff's head blossomed into view. Panicked, I destroyed the freshly lit cigarette and blew the smoke downwards.

"Couldn't help but hear you talking to yourself," he said with a smile. "It's okay. I do it once a week. Keeps the tools in the shed sharp, if you know what I mean."

"It's from a movie I saw," I tried to explain. "I just couldn't get the dialogue out of my mind."

Cliff stared at me intently from his side of the fence. "I'm starting to get offended."

"Come again?"

"Why do the Falcons think I'm an idiot?" Cliff asked. I blinked at him in surprise. "I had a whole conversation with myself about it yesterday," he continued. "You and your weird-ass husband. Heather, level with me. I know what you're going through."

I swallowed the panic rising in my throat. "It's a really good movie, Cliff. I'll let you borrow it. Don't tell anyone I was smoking."

He sighed, lowered himself briefly, then came back up to look at me. "What you got going on is an extremely overdue existential crisis. Let me give you an example."

"Sorry, Cliff. Nate needs me. He's—"

"Stop." Cliff held up a hand. "Don't return to old behavior patterns. That's a part of it. Right now, you're reverting."

"What?" I said it with a tinge of anger, feeling a little exposed.

"It's a fib, what you're telling me," Cliff said. "Want to know how I know that?"

"No. Okay." I attempted to repair the mashed cigarette by ripping off the top half and smoking the remains. "Go ahead."

"Before I moved here and eavesdropped on every conversation I could, I lived in a loft in Manhattan. I rose in a business comprised of snakes, backstabbers, coke addicts, and monsters. As a young man, I was king of them all. I married my high school sweetheart. Had three kids. And you know what happened next?"

"Clearly I don't," I said.

"The fucking market crashed." Cliff provided an example by flailing his arms and smacking his hands. "I self-destructed. Blamed the world. Lost my money. My wife, my kids. Everything. In the dark night of my soul, I asked myself: Would I trade my stock market brain for an easier life?"

"You worked on Wall Street?" I asked, surprised.

"Listen. You're like my damn kids. Listen"—he put his ear out toward me—"to what I'm saying. I had to come to terms with the fact that I am not what I do. I am not my money, my accolades, my status as a husband and father. My company, barely even my name. If I stripped it all away, at my core, I was simply a human. And that answer took me ten years to figure out. Now, I'm the new and improved Cliff. Not shackled by who I think I'm supposed to be."

I finished the half cigarette. "That's not really my problem. Enlightening for sure. And I appreciate you sharing it. But I don't think you understand what I'm going through."

Cliff gave me another look. "It's okay. You're not ready. I'll leave you with this. And *listen* to what I'm saying. Who you are, and who you think you are, are two entirely different people. Who you actually are, you don't want to be. So, you made up an imaginary person. Put on imaginary clothes, walked in an imaginary world. It's tough. I lost twenty pounds the night of my breakthrough. Only then is the voice in your head going to leave."

"I'm not crazy." Some emotion revealed itself through my eyes when I said the words.

Cliff smiled. "Neither am I."

Finally alone, I caressed the heart-shaped box. After digging in my pocket, I took out the diagnosis Dr. Morgan had written to me all those years ago. I dialed the number in her signature. The line was dead. I dialed another number. It rang.

"You've seen too much of me today, darling. Either things are really good, or the alternative," my mother answered.

"Do you have Dr. Morgan's number?"

There was a pause. "I can give you her daughter's."

". . . who followed in her mother's footsteps." I paused. "You ever wish I'd done that for you?"

There was a snort on the other end of the line. "You never could."

"Nail in the coffin."

"Not your fault. I'm a celestial being. Meaning, I walk on air."

LUDWIG

My hands began to hurt after fifteen minutes of smashing the smart lock on the front door. Angel unsuccessfully tried every pin combination and lock-picking technique in her repertoire of teenage skills. I dropped the frying pan for a moment and massaged my fingers.

"We're not using our heads. That's our problem. Like Kirk and Spock, we need to think this through," I said while sitting on the carpet. "Everything is sealed from the inside."

"How do smart locks work?" Angel asked.

"Honestly, either by the pin, biometrics, or the phone app. Maybe something like Google Home. Or . . ."

"Or what?" Angel asked.

"Maybe the batteries died?" I offered.

"The phone app idea sounds familiar to me."

"What's her number?" I picked up the old-fashioned-looking phone sitting on the table. "We can call from the landline."

"Right, because my brain is a database of numerical combinations. Wait, it's coming to me." Angel looked upward with two fingers on her temple, mocking me.

"555-867-5309. That's my mother's cell phone number. I memorized it the day she told me."

The flashback of us at the mall emerged. A symbiotic feeling of joy between us when she held the plastic-wrapped box. I was overflowing with pride because she had taken my suggestion. The smile she gave me from the teamwork we executed. It brought about the clearest picture of her face, now immortalized in my memory. I locked the moment in a special place. Normally it would go into the miscellaneous pile.

"Maybe I should just call her? Come to terms. My consciousness is tainted. Rides with strangers, drugged, assault on an old woman. Whose skull is remarkably resilient," I rambled.

"We Hernandezes are hardheaded," Angel said. "Between us, she's not my favorite aunt. I mean, I'm glad she's not dead. But I can cover this up. She had enemies. I'm gonna say it was a B and E."

"Why did you come here?"

She rubbed her arms slowly as if there were scars underneath. "Can I postpone my answer? Why did you run?"

I hesitated. "No real answer. All geniuses are cursed with common stupidity, I suppose."

"You're a little young for a genius. All we have to do is make it back to the train station. I have money. We just need to get out. Make it back."

I paused. "Do you know your social at least?"

Angel shrugged. "904, something something."

I sighed. There was no room left for placing blame or even frustration. Our eyes met briefly in the darkness of the room. A sliver of light from a passing car illuminated us both for a moment. In those brief seconds, I decided she was my friend from this point on.

"Plan B?" I stood up.

"No choice. Even though I'm pro-choice."

Summoning what strength I had left, I hurled the frying pan through the window. Angel took some cardboard and cleaned off shards of the remaining glass. I cupped my hands together and bent down for her to put her small foot into them and step up.

"You look good under me," Angel quipped before I boosted her out the window.

"Let's hope it doesn't rain."

The city air on my skin felt like a rebirth. I nearly prayed to the streetlight. Angel and I walked a few blocks before she reached into her bookbag and pulled out a cigarette. She offered me a stick of menthol death.

"Step one." She smiled before searching for a lighter.

"Step one of what?"

"Making up for the cell phone. That was my fault. I'm a big girl. I can admit that."

I waved the cigarette away. She shrugged her shoulders and lit hers. There was an eerie yellow brick road moment as we got closer to the train station. Everything around me felt dreamlike; some of the lights had tails, symptoms of exhaustion. Several well-to-do adults eyeballed us. Conspicuous ones in suits and lackadaisical ones searching for drugs. Angel flipped them off.

A couple of cars idled near us, crawling to a stop. A young girl smoking a cigarette was a mass text message to lunar perverts, rapists, and traffickers. As they stopped to speak to her, offering a ride, an unknown beast arose within me. Protective, like a dog. I hurled intellectual insults, flipped them off, and spat at the car as they drove off. Silently, we were a team.

"Do you really have a tattoo?" I mumbled the words a little bit. "Of a tiger? Or was that a rumor?"

"Near my subsection?" She rolled her eyes. "Maybe."

"I don't care. It's just, my mind gets scatterbrained when I'm tired. It's all regurgitated knowledge."

"After a few dates—"

"How clichéd."

She skipped in front of me and began to walk backward. "You know what made me like you, Ludwig?"

It felt like a trick question, but I fell right into the trap anyway. "The fact that my IQ is over 130? My hidden talent of juggling knives? Butter knives only. My expansive essay on Schrödinger's cat?"

"No, it's—"

"Oh, I also can recite the entire Transformers song, 'You Got the Touch' by the great artist Stan Bush, circa 1986, in German. Du hast die Beruhrung—"

"No." Angel laughed. "It's because you are entirely yourself. A one of one. It's rare. I'm like five people. Six on the weekends."

"So who are you now?"

"Olive juice."

I stared at her for a moment. "I still don't know what that means."

"Doesn't matter."

I saw the gleaming lights from the shitty train station. My mouth was salivating at the prospect of the overly priced goods inside. The smell of urine on the steps. The rocking of the locomotive that would lull me to sleep. The comfort of not being alone. The reunion of my room, my parents. Whom I genuinely missed, in every sense of the word.

NATHANIEL

The vodka-turned-water replenished my hands from the manic writing session. Three thousand words in one sitting. A sober best. Dexterity was nearly gone when I operated my cell phone.

"What you doing?" My question was full of off-putting vibrancy. Signals that symbolized change or self-destruction. "Masturbating?"

"Close. Reading *White Fang*," my brother said.

"Pause it. Got my update. You have to read this."

"Stop reading Jack London for your masterpiece?" I heard him tapping a pen. "Stop Jack London for your great American novel? Sold. Send it over."

"Sending it now. Wait. You're not going to read it, are you?"

"This conversation has peaked."

As he hung up, I stood from my chair. Surrounded by trinkets and relics of who I used to be ashamed of. I breathed in deeply to cushion my soul. For another hour I relived as many memories as my mind could conjure. I remembered reading my little brother's first spec script. I was jealous of his wordplay. The carefulness of his plot. The last sentence I wrote in my own screenplay before I abandoned the craft and tossed the tablet into a pool of water.

I opened a new document, wrote down the dream in as much detail as I could, compared it to the manuscript. As the cursor rested on the word *father*, I stared into the screen before backspacing it all away. Heather yelled something incoherent from the other room. I ignored it.

The blank page mocked me. I saved the emptiness. *Breathe deeply*, I told myself, venturing into a poor man's meditation. I closed my eyes, drifted into the nuances of my story for ten seconds. Quickly, my subconscious washed it away, replaced it with my dad in different stages of his life. From when he appeared as a giant to a shriveled, mean old man grasping my hand with an IV needle taped below his knuckles. Creativity left the room. Triggers entered. I followed. Returned to my wife.

Heather was sitting on the edge of the bed, hanging up a call. When she looked at me, I saw someone new.

"I'm making an appointment."

"Pregnant?" My stomach clenched at the thought. Ludwig was almost an adult; was I about to be saddled with another responsibility?

"With a therapist."

I let the silence grow before I responded. "Everything okay?"

"Yea. You?"

I shrugged. "Weird weekend, and it's only Saturday"

"Feels longer than that when it's just us," she acknowledged.

"I want to call him, but—"

"Nah, let him be." My wife waved a hand. "No news is good news."

"Yea."

"You sure everything's good, right?" I asked. "Because I'm going to run to the store real quick. Unless you need me here."

"Getting something to drink?"

"Yea."

She turned away. "Grab me some wine while you're out."

"No problem."

Before I stepped into the hallway, she called out in a soft tone. "That scene, when you woke up on the floor. I won't tell anybody."

"I already forgot about it."

Pulling into the convenience store, turning the wheel wide as I do by habit, I slid into the same parking spot I always managed to get. Near the entrance, dressed in a children's coat peppered with stains, straggly hair covering her beady eyes, was an old friend. The drunk woman waved at me; half sane, half crazy. I nodded back. We had a rapport. We both drank from the same poisonous chalice. A jingle of bells above the door upon my entrance. I was met with waves of "Heys." A local celebrity.

The embrace felt like puncture wounds, hitting places with the least muscle mass. Without acknowledging them, I perused the aisles. Sauvignon blanc for Heather was obtained. Another patron, comrade in arms, greeted me from the parallel aisle. I forced a smile before returning to my home plate. All the logos on the bottles. The keys. I rubbed my throat, grabbed the bottle.

At the register, a clerk full of cheer. She leaned near the carved-out bulletproof window. "Buy more, Nate. We might be getting shut down," she said.

"That's all government bullshit. Population control! They were trying to stop Hong Kong and it spread. Like AIDS!" a random customer yelled. I couldn't see his face.

"Don't no one want to hear your two cents, Tommy," the female clerk said as she reached below the countertop, pulled out a Ziploc bag full of masks. "For you and yours. Be safe out here."

"No hazmat suit?" I smiled.

"It's on backorder." She smiled.

I carefully placed the clanking bottles on the floor of the back seat. As the car started, I felt a bit of wind on the back of my neck. When I adjusted my rearview mirror, I saw him in the back seat, my dead father.

"Hate and love, baby boy. All the same."

"I need to drive." I turned away, but his voice continued.

"If it makes you feel better, I can move to the front seat?"

I pulled into the street. Two car horns blared at me. Nearly sideswiped a minivan.

"This is how you end me?" I asked. "Driving sober, fifteen minutes from my house. Well played, sir."

"I can't kill what's already dead," he said.

"Maybe I can resurrect if I bury myself in the backyard? What's it like down there?"

"Hell or the coffin?"

"Whichever one I'm headed to," I said.

"It's an aerial view of the person's life by the one who thinks about you the most."

"Anything else before I T-bone?"

"Keep the wine," he advised. "And only the wine."

Traffic built up on the main road. More cars than usual, even for this time of day. Early panickers. I saw an opening made for carnage. I put on my blinker. Speeding up, I dove into the fray, hearing tires screech behind me. I pressed on. Hit the concrete, kept going. The tires were still good. Slowed down. Got out of the car. Kissed the key on the bottle. Placed it on the curb. Drove home.

HEATHER

I couldn't get an appointment. Her office was closed for an indeterminate amount of time. I found myself back in Ludwig's room, smelling my son's scent. I opened his "Do not read" journal again, fished out a pen from the garbage on his computer desk.

After writing in the date on the last page, I allowed my mind to compel my fingers and I confessed:

> *You may have what I have. It won't be exactly like my story. For you, it could be now. I survived it. Well, I'm surviving it. You will too. It's all about believing in a trusting voice. An external voice. Not your own. You will find it dazzling and terrifying out there. Hopefully, you will find a woman who loves you the way Nate loves me. An imperfect love. A balance of the imbalanced.*
>
> *I see things, Son. Your grandfather saw things. Things that aren't there. It will never go away. I will never heal from it. I will never medicate. I could use a person to talk to. I nominate you to be my trusting voice. To tell me when I'm drifting.*

> *To anchor me in the torrential waves of my imagination. I can die that way. That's all I want from you. I don't care about the grades, the manners, the achievements. At your core, that's already there. I want you to fail, so you learn how to win. Promise me when you read this, at whatever time it is, that you will come find me. Hug me, and tell me: ok somno suo ad ire.*

I signed it with a tear. Rose began a slow clap, legs crossed in the wicker chair half the size of the room. She lowered her head with her eyes on me before wrapping her arms around the Tibetan sound bowl. Then, she bent down and put her face inside. The instrument became an animal, swallowing her whole. The chair empty. I closed the book in amazement. Stood. Sat. Stood again, peeked inside the bowl. I saw a miniature universe of luminous stars: verdant, crimson, and cobalt. A falling comet striking the center. Planets rotating around a gigantic black hole.

"Rose?"

LUDWIG

Her head bobbed on my shoulder as the locomotive buckled on the tracks. Drool pooled down my sweaty shirt. I felt drunk from tiredness. Multiple times I stopped myself from caressing her hair, but I snuck kisses on her forehead at every stop. Every time the train conductor yelled through the speakers, she responded with a heavy exhale. And every time a new person walked through our car.

The miniature television set up in the corner blared COVID-19 messages over and over. On a heat map of America, I saw my state in bright orange. The ticker across the bottom said: *Quarantine in effect for certain states. More to come.* I tuned out mentally.

All the lies I conjured to tell my mother about the missing cell phone. The never-to-be-had adventures I shared with Ace. The fake meals his mother made. All the bullshit stories his father rehearsed after reading the paper. I sighed. I've grown. Enough to share . . . with her. Never him.

Angel snorted, coughed, opened her red eyes, blinked, put her head back down on my shoulder. She felt safe there. Two people plopped into the seats behind us. A hand fell on my shoulder.

"Find yourself?" Alo asked.

"Hey . . ." I stretched out the sound. "I remember you. And you. And you. And you?"

All four of them were sitting in pairs across from each other. Dead on one side, alive, I believed, on the other.

"He's not coming back," the girl in the bikini said.

The smile that took over my face went beyond the borders of my cheeks. "Why did you get on the train? Don't you have a vehicle?"

"Kindred spirits." The bell-bottoms man laughed.

"Don't be mean," Shaya butted in. "You did the best you could. Better than sleeping under that bridge."

"Yea, I suppose so," I answered without fully grasping the gravity of the situation.

"You ran off with your friend, I see. She's a malaikat," Alo replied.

"I'm not ashamed to admit I don't know what that is," I answered, still smiling. "But I happen to be fond of this mally cat." Her hair felt like water when I finally ran my hand through it.

"This is your story. Just how you wanted it," Shaya declared.

"At one point you left me on a filthy couch on the sidewalk," I said. "Drugged."

"We educated you. You never left the room," the bikini woman interjected, shaking the flip-flops on her feet.

"Come again?"

"He's not ready. Kindred spirits," bell-bottoms repeated.

"Why do you keep saying that?"

"LAST STOP!" the train conductor blared through the overhead speakers.

I shuddered myself awake. Angel wasn't by my side. In her place was my bookbag. Outside, the sun seemed threatening. I touched the glass to feel a sensation on my fingers.

"Where am I?" A panicked whisper came out of my mouth. "Is this?"

A smaller, softer hand fell on my shoulder. I gripped it hard.

"I left you this time," Angel said.

It took a moment longer than normal to recognize reality. "I won't do it again," I replied.

ACKNOWLEDGEMENTS

I found writing screenplays difficult, but these experiences pushed me into writing fiction. My wife, Laneta, was the first to encourage me to write in the book format. It turned out I had written about 70 pages with ease. This gave me the fire to see if I could finish a whole novel. Which I have now done four times.

A shoutout to Drunk Monkeys for being the first publication to take a chance on me. When they published my short story, "The Gauntlet," I knew I was onto something. Special thanks to Jamil, my brother, and fellow writer Pierre Boodhoo not only for reading all my crazy drafts, but for letting me get all these weird, incomplete ideas out of my head in our long late-night conversations. Thanks to my friend Erik Council who created the graphics for my first novel - dead cheap. Lastly, my thanks to The Fictional Cafe for making me feel my writing was worth publishing, and especially my editor, Jack B. Rochester, who genuinely liked my writing style even though I was always going outside the box and switching genres as frequently as possible. I wouldn't be here without you, Jack.

About the Author

Derrick R. Lafayette has written four novels and over a dozen short stories, published in print and online. He was The Fictional Café's 2021-2022 Writer-in-Residence. When he's not working as an IT engineer or studying chess gambits on the astral plane, he's reading or writing profusely. You can find more of his work on <u>Amazon</u>.

CPSIA information can be obtained
at www.ICGtesting.com
Printed in the USA
BVHW071315060423
661868BV00008B/488

9 780984 036998